P9-CNB-853
Performance Pavilion
Gazebo
Annika's house
K
Kommissary
GS headquarters
CAMPUS GROUNDS
N
W
E
S

The Bad Apple

MERITS OF MISCHIEF

The Bad Apple

T. R. BURNS

Aladdin

New York London Toronto Sydney New Delhi

This book is a work of fiction. Any references to historical events, real people, or real locales are used fictitiously. Other names, characters, places, and incidents are the product of the author's imagination, and any resemblance to actual events or locales or persons, living or dead, is entirely coincidental.

ALADDIN
An imprint of Simon & Schuster Children's Publishing Division
1230 Avenue of the Americas, New York, NY 10020
First Aladdin hardcover edition April 2012

Designed by Karina Granda
The text of this book was set in Bembo.
Manufactured in the United States of America 0312 FFG
2 4 6 8 10 9 7 5 3 1
Library of Congress Cataloging-in-Publication Data
Burns, T. R., 1978–
The bad apple / T. R. Burns.
p. cm. — (Merits of mischief ; 1)
Summary: After accidentally killing a substitute teacher with an apple, twelve-year-old Seamus Hinkle is sent to Kilter Academy, where, in order to excel as he always has, he must behave badly and pull pranks on his teachers, but along with new friends Lemon and Elinor he discovers that there is more to the Academy than meets the eye.
ISBN 978-1-4424-4029-6 (hc)
[1. Behavior—Fiction. 2. Boarding schools—Fiction. 3. Schools—Fiction. 4. Tricks—Fiction. 5. Humorous stories.] I. Title.
PZ7.B937455Bad 2012
[Fic]—dc23
2011042333
ISBN 978-1-4424-4031-9 (eBook)

For Rebecca

Acknowledgments

This tale never could have been tattled without the help of some very mischievous miscreants, rabble-rousers, and other assorted troublemakers. For all they do to spread lies—cleverly disguised as "stories"—throughout the world, I must thank Rebecca Sherman, Liesa Abrams, Mara Anastas, Jenna Shaw, and everyone at Writers House and Aladdin/Simon & Schuster. For training me in the ways of trouble at a very young age, I wasn't then, but am now, extremely grateful to my siblings, Sean and Kristin. The same goes for Mom, who was, for better or worse, the best trouble-busting Good Samaritan a kid could ask for. I must also thank misbehaving Michael and the rest of my friends and family, who could probably pool their demerits and start their own top secret troublemaking academy. If they do, I'll be sure to tell you.

Or will I?

You might just have to act up to find out.

The Bad Apple

Chapter 1

At exactly 11:17 every Fish Stick Tuesday, I raise my hand in algebra class and make a very important announcement.

"Seamus Hinkle," Mr. McGill will say, peering at me over the tops of his dusty glasses. "To what do I owe the honor?"

"I need to use the restroom," I'll say.

"I need to go on a permanent tropical vacation. Is there a pass for that?"

This is Mr. McGill's idea of a joke. Not bad, considering he's a math teacher who memorizes pi for fun.

"The period's almost over," he'll continue. "Don't worry about coming back."

And this is my idea of the perfect response. Mr. McGill never seems to recall that we've had the same exact conversation many times before, and neither do my classmates. Sometimes I think it'd be nice to be more memorable, but on Tuesday mornings, it's always better to be forgotten.

My routine goes off without a hitch, week after week, until Mr. McGill drops his favorite calculator while taking a bubble bath. According to the e-mail he sends all his students, the calculator no longer multiplies. So he takes the day off to repair it.

And we get a substitute.

Her name's Miss Parsippany. She has curly blond hair, big blue eyes, and a bad case of first-day jitters. By 10:45 she's dropped—and broken—eight pieces of chalk. At 10:57 she claps two erasers together to clean them and is nearly suffocated by a thick white cloud. At 11:09 she asks for help setting up the laptop projector, and when no one volunteers, she plugs the inside corners of her eyes with her pinkie and thumb to keep them from leaking.

I feel bad for her, but I'm also encouraged by her fragile emotional state. Every second counts on Fish Stick Tuesdays, so at 11:15—two minutes ahead of schedule—I raise my hand.

"Oh." Miss Parsippany grabs the edge of the desk when she sees me, like she's afraid of falling down. "You have a question?"

"I need to use the restroom," I say.

"But there are"—she sifts through a stack of papers, many of which slip from her grasp and float to the floor—"seven minutes left in this period."

I grab my backpack and start to stand. "Don't worry. I'll just go to lunch from there."

"You can't."

I stop. Miss Parsippany's watching me, her blue eyes wide, her mouth partially open. At first I think she's about to be sick in Mr. McGill's circular file, but then her eyes relax and her mouth closes.

"You can't," she says again, her voice firmer.

"But I always do. This time, every Tuesday."

Her eyebrows lower. "You have to use the restroom at the same time every Tuesday?"

To someone who actually pays attention, I can see how this might sound strange.

"You *do*," a low voice says somewhere behind me. "Why is that?"

"Little kid, little bladder," another voice says, making the room swell with whispers and giggles.

I know those voices. The kids they belong to are the same ones I'm trying to outrun.

"Please," I say as my face burns. "I really have to go."

"Well, I'm sorry. You've made it this long, you can make it another few minutes."

Just my luck. Saying no to me is the one thing for which Miss Parsippany feels qualified.

I stand there, unsure what to do. Part of me is tempted to bolt for the door, but a bigger part locks my feet in place.

So I drop back into my chair. I watch the second hand click around the wall clock. And at 11:19 and forty-five seconds, I throw my backpack onto my shoulders and crouch above my seat, one foot in the aisle.

The bell rings. I run—and am immediately stalled by a gaggle of girls. I veer to the left, but the girl on that end flips her hair over her shoulder, and it catches me in the eye. I veer to the right, but the girl on that end is texting and keeps swerving into the narrow open space between her and the wall. I try slipping between the girls in the middle, but they're packed tightly together, as if connected by their shiny belts and silver hoop earrings.

Eventually, they make a slow turn toward the courtyard, and I dart past them. I move as quickly as I can, but the hallway's crowded. By the time the cafeteria comes into view, it's already 11:25—and I'm four minutes behind schedule.

I burst through the doors and then stop short. It's even worse than I feared. There are at least thirty kids in line—thirty kids I should be in front of. That's why I leave math early every Tuesday, to get a head start.

And bringing up the rear is my biggest enemy, my arch-nemesis, my worst nightmare—at least on Monday nights.

Bartholomew John.

He's everything I'm not. Tall. Strong. Able to talk himself out of trouble despite a seriously stunted vocabulary. In fact, there's only one thing in the entire world that Bartholomew John and I have in common.

Fish sticks.

Not just any fish sticks. The kind Lady Lorraine and the kitchen crew of Cloudview Middle School make, with crunchy outsides, flaky insides, and an aftertaste that lasts for days.

"Want a boost?" Alex Ortiz, Bartholomew John's sidekick, asks when I come up behind them. He puts one hand on top of the other, palms up, and squats.

"Or a rocket launcher?" Bartholomew John adds without turning around.

I'm standing on my toes to survey the situation up ahead and now drop to my heels. I don't answer them. They don't expect me to. We all know that's not how this works.

It takes eleven agonizing minutes to reach the lunch counter. I try not to stress by focusing on the comforting aromas of grease and salt, but that only reminds me of what I'll likely be missing.

"It's fish stick day?" Bartholomew John asks loudly when he's next in line. "Alex, did *you* know it was fish stick day?"

"Nope. What an unexpected surprise."

This exchange is for my benefit. There was an unfortunate incident a few weeks ago, at the beginning of the school year, when Bartholomew John loaded his plate with the last of the fish sticks and I tried to swipe some from his tray. In true Bartholomew John style, he made a big fuss by telling Lady Lorraine, the cafeteria monitors, and eventually the principal that I came up out of nowhere and shoved him aside to steal his food. For extra sympathy points, he added that his family couldn't afford to go out to eat and that he saved his meager allowance to buy lunch as a special treat.

Never mind that if I tried shoving him aside the force would send me crashing to the floor. Or that both his parents are lawyers. His lie got me after-school detention for the first time ever. The only good thing about the whole situation was that Bartholomew John seemed to forget about it, until today.

Darn that Miss Parsippany.

"This batch is extra yummy," Lady Lorraine says, sliding a spatula through the tray. "Got distracted by a rat the size of Texas and forgot I had 'em in the fryer."

"Fantastic." Bartholomew John grabs the fish sticks she scoops on his plate and shoves them in his mouth.

My chest tightens as she gives him another serving, and another, and another. He clears his plate as fast as she fills it. I manage not to panic until the slick bottom of the tray appears, and then a hot heat shoots from my head to my toes, like I've just been dipped in Lady Lorraine's fish fryer.

"There's more where that came from," she says when the tray's empty.

I fan my face with a stack of napkins. Bartholomew John belches. The sound's gross but reassuring; I've learned from past experience that as delicious as they are, there are only so many fish sticks one human stomach can handle.

"This is it until next week." Lady Lorraine drops a new tray on the counter.

"Is it fat?"

I tear my gaze away from the fish sticks and look at Alex's finger, which is pointing to a corner of the kitchen.

"And hairy?" Alex continues. "With a tail that could lasso everyone in this room?"

"It is," Lady Lorraine says grimly. She tears off her hairnet, grabs a spatula, and spins around.

For a second, I actually believe Alex saw a rat. I'm so busy watching Lady Lorraine creep toward the empty corner that I almost miss what Bartholomew John does next.

He takes a carton of milk. Opens it. And empties it over the remaining fish sticks.

"Calcium." He crushes the carton in one fist and tosses it on my tray. "Helps you grow."

I stare at the milk carton. I want to pick it up and hurl it at him, but I know it won't do any good. Instead I slide my tray past the soggy fish and take my only remaining options: a salad and an apple.

In the cafeteria I sit at an empty table in the back of the room. I take a notebook and pencil from my backpack, push my tray aside, and start a list.

HOW TO GET REVENGE ON FISH HEAD

1. Start another list of—

That's as far as I get before a commotion on the other side of the room makes me look up. Bartholomew John and Alex are standing inches away from three members of the boys' soccer team. They're all yelling at the same time, so I can't tell what they're arguing about, but I see Bartholomew John shove the team captain, who shoves him back. Alex throws a low punch at another kid, who punches him back. Soon fists and limbs are flying, and students and teachers swarm toward the fight from around the cafeteria.

Troublemakers, I think. Hoping Bartholomew John gets what's coming, I climb on top of my chair for a better view.

And then I see her. Miss Parsippany. Pushing through the crowd.

She's going to try to stop them. She managed to say no to me, and now she thinks she can break up a brawl that even the biggest male teachers are afraid to get near.

I usually don't act without significant forethought, but there's no time for that now. Keeping my eye on Bartholomew John, I snatch the apple from my lunch tray, bring my arm all the way back, and fling it forward.

In the next instant, the fight's over.

And Miss Parsippany's on the floor.

Chapter 2

I killed her.

Some people say it was an accident. They say I didn't mean to do it, that I was just scared and tried to help. That may be true. But what's also true is that Miss Parsippany, who'd been a substitute teacher for all of four hours and thirteen minutes, was alive in homeroom and dead by lunch.

Because of me.

Which is why, less than a week later, my mother, father, and I are driving north—far north, like, wave-hello-to-Santa-and-his-elves north—to the Kilter Academy for Troubled Youth.

"How you doing back there, sport?" Dad asks at the top of hour seven. "Need anything?"

"Eliot," Mom says. "Please stay focused."

"Judith," Dad says. "I am focused. I was merely asking Seamus if—"

"What Seamus needs is to be on time. And what I need is for you to read signs so we don't miss our turn."

Dad settles back in the passenger seat. I know he's trying to catch my eye in the side-view mirror, but I keep looking out my window. The last thing I deserve right now is sympathy.

Trees grow taller, closer together. Buildings disappear. The road goes from straight and flat to steep and curvy. The pressure clogs my ears and muffles the sound of tires whirring across pavement. I squeeze my nose between my thumb and pointer finger, prepared to blow, but then I catch Mom's lips moving out of the corner of my eye and change my mind.

The pressure builds as we climb higher. It feels like two very large hands are wringing my head like a wet towel. I see white spots, then red.

Eventually, the car lurches to a stop. My ears pop. The spots vanish.

"Naptime's over."

I open my eyes to see Mom standing next to my door. Behind her is a chain-link fence topped with barbed wire. Behind the fence is a gray, windowless brick building.

We're here.

Mom heads for the gate, and I put on my shoes and gather my books.

"It's so quiet," I say as I slide out of the car.

"I think it's kind of nice." Dad comes up next to me and rests one hand on top of my head. "Serene. Peaceful."

We stand there a second, listening. The school's surrounded by woods, but they don't make a sound. Leaves don't rustle, birds don't sing, the air doesn't stir. No other cars drive up next to ours. I'm about to ask if we made a mistake, if maybe there's another Kilter Academy for Troubled Youth, one closer to a mall and gas stations and other signs of life, when the front gate screams open.

Still on top of my head, Dad's hand twitches.

"It's okay," I lie. "I'll be okay."

Mom's already halfway down the front path, so I start jogging to catch up. I look around as I go, taking in the yellow grass, patches of mud, and white sky. I rub my arms, not sure whether the goose bumps are from nerves or the cold. Back home, it was sixty degrees and sunny, a typical fall day. Here, it looks and feels like late winter, when the ground's just beginning to thaw but a sudden snowstorm could still pack another icy punch. It's almost uncomfortable enough to make me want to go inside.

Almost.

"Remember," Mom says when I reach her, "this place is the best. You will do what they say. Are we clear?"

"Yes," I say, still jogging to keep her pace. "I promise I'll—"

"Promise?" a voice booms overhead.

Mom stops short. I'm following close behind and swerve to the side to avoid a collision.

"It's a little late for that, don't you think?"

I look up at the closed gray doors, then over my shoulder. Whoever's speaking sounds near enough to yell in our ears . . . but there's no one there.

"At the Kilter Academy for Troubled Youth," the voice continues, "we see and hear everything. You might want to keep that in mind."

"Security cameras." Mom nods to a small black box above the doorway. "Of course."

She waves to the camera and hurries up the stairs. I start after her, but my feet are heavier, slower now. I've moved only two steps when the gray doors open and a woman appears.

At least, I think a woman appears. From the neck down she looks more like a man than every woman—and most men—I've met. She's wearing dark green pants, a matching long-sleeve shirt that buttons all the way up her neck, and black leather boots laced so tightly my calves pulsate in sympathy. Of course, her calves are probably fine; they're big and sharp, just like her quads, biceps, shoulders, and even her wrists. There must be spandex in her uniform, because if there wasn't, her muscles would rip it to shreds the second she stepped away from her closet. I wouldn't be surprised if underneath her clothes, her skin's green too.

"If you're waiting for a written invitation, you're going to be waiting a very long time." The voice, which belongs to her, also sounds more manly than not.

"This is Ms. Kilter," Mom says when I reach the top step.

"It's nice to meet you," I mumble just as Dad comes up behind us. He's moving slowly, dragging my duffel bag behind him. When he reaches the top step, he wipes his wet forehead and takes a deep breath.

"What a lovely facility," he says, like the gray building is an old Victorian and Ms. Kilter's clipboard is a tray of blueberry muffins.

Too nervous to move, I wait until Dad's close enough, then hold out one hand to take the duffel bag.

We head inside, single-file. The lobby reminds me of my orthodontist's lobby, except that it doesn't have plants, magazines, or a fish tank. It doesn't have any couches or chairs, either; the only furniture is a small wooden desk in the middle of the room and an empty coatrack.

A closed, unmarked door is on the far wall. Bad things—braces, retainers, all kinds of torture—happen behind doors like that.

"Personal effects," Ms. Kilter barks.

I look down. The beam of sunlight coming from the front door, which is still open, disappears under a metal bin.

"Your stuff," Mom prompts. "It needs to be screened."

Screened. For knives, guns, bombs. Because that's what criminals carry, just like other people carry cell phones and breath mints.

I place my backpack and duffel bag in the bin. I want to ask if I'll get them back, but don't.

Ms. Kilter lifts the bin with one hand and tosses it on her shoulder like it's filled with feathers. She crosses the room, slides a long drawer out from the far wall, and drops in the bin. A few seconds later, there's a loud clang.

"That'll do it." She bumps the drawer closed with her hip. "Do you need directions back to the highway?"

"That's it?"

Ms. Kilter turns to me, eyebrows raised.

"I'm sorry," I say, only slightly aware of the blood leaving my face. "It's just, we've been here five minutes and—"

What about the tour? Orientation? Lunch? Or at the very least, paperwork?

"This isn't summer camp," Mom reminds me. "If you wanted to be treated like a good kid, maybe you should've acted like one."

She's said this before, like when I lost TV privileges for forgetting to make my bed three days in a row. Or when she hid my video games after one too many late-night sessions made me fall asleep at breakfast. But it sounds different now. It *feels* different—kind of like a fist to my stomach. Which is why I look down and focus on breathing.

"Don't worry, Mrs. Hinkle. By the time we're done with him, your son will be so well behaved you'll wonder if he's the same one you left here today."

As if to prove her point, Ms. Kilter pats her waist—where handcuffs and a black holster hang from a thick leather belt.

"I'm not worried," Mom says with a small smile. "Not anymore."

She faces me. I try to make my eyes meet hers, but can't. Staring at the floor, I see the tips of her shoes near the toes of my sneakers, and my heart lifts. She's going to hug me. Yes, she's mad, and sad, and disappointed. Yes, she's going to leave me here, all alone, for the next three months. But she still loves me. She's not giving up on me. We're going to get through this and be a family again—maybe even a better one than we were before.

She leans toward me—so close I can smell this morning's coffee on her breath. When she speaks, her voice is barely a whisper.

"Make me proud, Seamus," she says, then grabs me in a quick, tight hug.

I open my mouth to promise I'll try, but she's out the door before I can find the words.

"Stay strong, sport." Dad throws his arms around me and pulls me close. His belly jiggles against my chest, and I know he's fighting tears. "And remember what I always say. If someone's not being nice . . ."

His voice fades, and now I'm fighting tears too. Because what Dad always says, what he always *said*, was, *If someone's not being nice, kill them with kindness.* But he can't say that anymore.

Somewhere outside, Mom calls for him. He presses his face into my hair, kisses the top of my head, and releases me.

I watch him leave, a blur of khaki and yellow plaid. He pulls the front doors closed behind him, careful not to look at me again.

The doors click. Sunlight vanishes. A moment later, a car starts.

It was an accident.

Of course it was. I see it all perfectly now—fists flying, lunch trays sliding, Miss Parsippany falling, clutching her head with both hands. It was a terrible, tragic accident that everyone will understand once I explain. That they'll forgive, once I apologize.

"I'm sorry," I whisper.

Beneath me, my feet begin moving.

"I'm sorry," I say, louder.

My feet move faster. Soon I'm running, sprinting, flinging the door open.

"I'm sorry!"

The car's already pulling away from the curb. My breath catches when the taillights flicker red. I start to step through the doorway—and am instantly yanked back.

"I wouldn't do that if I were you," Ms. Kilter says quietly near my ear.

It's good advice.

Especially since she's holding a gun to my neck.

Chapter 3

Please—don't shoot. I'll do whatever you say, I promise."

"There's that word again." She digs the gun in deeper. "Wave."

"What?"

"Your parents. They won't leave unless they know everything's under control. Let them know it is."

I don't feel good lying on top of everything else, but I don't have much of a choice. I try to keep my chin from trembling as

I raise one hand. My fingers aren't even fully extended when the taillights dim and the car continues down the driveway.

"Good." She lowers the gun and releases my arm. "Thirsty?"

Her voice sounds different now, lighter. I turn around slowly, terrified that it's a ploy to lower my defenses and better her aim. The terror increases when she smiles at me—and then points the gun at her open mouth.

"Don't!"

I lunge for the weapon just as she pulls the trigger. A stream of water flies from the barrel and lands at the back of her throat.

"Want a hit?" she asks.

Stepping back, I look at the gun, then at her. "No, thank you." I hardly hear the words over my heart, which pounds in my ears.

"Polite." She nods. "Just like your father said."

She turns and heads inside, leaving me in the open doorway. It's clear I'm supposed to follow, but why didn't she close and lock the door first? She's already halfway across the room and not even looking back. It would be easy to make a break for it.

But the front yard must be booby-trapped. The second I step outside, a hidden grenade will detonate, taking my feet with it. And a hundred security guards are probably watching nearby,

just waiting for me to make a wrong move so they can attack. That has to be how Mom was able to keep me out of juvenile detention, by promising to lock me up somewhere worse.

"Shall we?"

I pull the heavy doors closed and turn around. It takes a second for my eyes to adjust to the low light coming from the small desk lamp. When they do, I think I see Ms. Kilter standing by the door on the far wall, and then need another second to decide if it's really her. The military-like uniform has been replaced with white leggings and a long, gray top that's not quite a dress and not quite a shirt. Instead of black boots she wears shiny silver flats. Her dark brown hair, which had been pulled back in a tight knot, hangs loose past her shoulders.

"Yes, Ms. Kilter," I say carefully, just to make sure.

She smiles. "That sounds so formal, doesn't it? Why don't you call me by my first name?"

Isn't that one of the main things adults really like about being adults? The right to be addressed respectfully, as "Mr.," "Mrs.," or "Ms.," followed by their last names? This must be another trick designed to make me relax enough to fall into other Kilter traps.

"It's okay, Seamus." She walks to the middle of the room and

holds out one hand. "I'm Annika. It's a pleasure to meet you."

I scan the room without moving my head, expecting someone—someone big, strong, and armed with something far more dangerous than a water gun—to jump out from the shadows and yell, "Gotcha!"

But no one does. So I shuffle to the middle of the room and take her hand. It's warm and soft.

"Would you like to see your room?" Annika asks. Not waiting for an answer, she returns to the door on the far wall and stands next to it as I pass through.

I step outside and stop short. "I think I'm in the wrong place."

"Actually," Annika says, "you're exactly where you're supposed to be."

She must have me confused with someone else. I should be someplace like the Kilter Academy lobby, only smaller, darker, with no furniture or exits. But on the other side of the door, there's lush green grass. Flowers. Fountains and statues. A stone path that weaves toward another building, partially hidden by blooming vines.

"Is it to remind me of what I'll be missing once I'm locked up?" I ask.

She smiles. "Your father said you were polite. He didn't

mention you were funny." And then she starts down the path.

I hurry after her, my fear eased slightly by curiosity. The path is long, and the building it leads to farther away than it initially appeared. There's plenty of time to notice other differences between this outdoor area and the front yard, like the warmer air and birds flitting overhead. I wonder if Mom skipped this part in the Kilter Academy promotional video. If she'd seen it, she'd never have signed me up.

We cut through the garden and enter a second, newer building with floor-to-ceiling windows. Inside, Annika leads me down a hallway. "There's the Adrenaline Pavilion," she says.

I follow her nod to the windows and another outdoor area. This one has an in-ground pool, basketball courts, volleyball courts, a baseball diamond, a track, and an enormous wooden jungle gym. All are empty.

"There's the media room."

I slow down as we pass a large room with glass walls. Inside are tall shelves lined with DVDs, the biggest flat-screen TV I've ever seen . . . and my fellow criminals, sprawled across couches and armchairs. They stare silently at the TV, clearly mesmerized by the six-foot-tall Frodo running on-screen.

"You'll meet everyone at dinner," Annika calls back.

My stomach flip-flops. It's nice to know I'm not alone, but I don't really need to make friends. Who knows why these kids are here?

"Speaking of dinner," Annika says when I reach her. "Fish sticks?"

"I'm sorry?"

"Fish sticks." She stops in front of a light green door. "Crunchy on the outside, flaky on the inside. With an aftertaste that lasts for days. Your favorite, right?"

My heart shoots toward my throat. Of course. It all makes sense. Getting out of juvie. Mom and Dad leaving so quickly. The beautiful gardens, elaborate playground, larger-than-life-size *Lord of the Rings*. Fish sticks.

There's only one reason a place like this cooks a murderer his favorite meal.

Because it's his last.

"Oh, good," Annika says cheerfully. "Lemon's up."

She knocks on the light green door. When it opens, I realize the pounding bass that's making the floor vibrate beneath my feet isn't coming from my chest. It's coming from two small orbs inside the room.

"Welcome home!"

At least, I think that's what Annika says. The music—if that's what you can call the banging drums and screaming synthesizer—is so loud I have to read her lips.

She keeps talking, but I stop reading to look around. The room is twice the size of my real bedroom, with walls the same color as the door and a wood floor covered by a round ivory area rug. Tall windows look out onto a rolling field. There are two beds, dressers, and desks. A kid sits at one of the desks with his back to us.

Lemon, Annika mouths, and points.

His head is lowered, like he's reading or writing and deep in concentration. He doesn't acknowledge us. He might not even know we're here, since the speakers are pumping right next to his left elbow. Annika goes over to him, looks at whatever he's working on, and gives him an approving smile. She points at me and says my name, which makes his head tilt up . . . but then it drops again.

Her smile doesn't falter as she comes back to me. She brings an imaginary fork to her mouth and mimes eating, then holds up six fingers.

Apparently, my last dinner is at six o'clock.

I'm not sure what to do when she leaves. My duffel bag and backpack are on one of the beds, but what's the point in unpacking? *The Fellowship of the Ring* is my favorite movie, but what's the point in watching? The only thing I'd like to do is talk to my parents, to tell them I'm sorry one last time, but they probably don't want to hear from me.

The room grows hazy. I think I'm on the verge of passing out from stress and start for the bed . . . but then I smell something.

Smoke.

It's coming from Lemon's desk. It drifts to the ceiling in white wisps, and quickly turns gray, then black.

His head stays lowered, but his shoulders rise and fall.

Did he fall asleep? Dad likes to do the Sunday crossword puzzle with a single candle lit for ambience. Was Lemon writing by a lit candle that he accidentally knocked over when—

"What are you *doing*?" I yell.

Now by his desk, I know what he's not doing: sleeping. He's blowing on the small fire in front of him, which grows taller with every puff.

There's a watercooler in the corner of the room. I bolt toward it, fill two cups, and return to the desk. The sizzle of extinguishing flames can be heard between drumbeats.

Lemon sits back. He stares at the wet, black pile in front of him, and then slowly looks up.

He's about my age, with shaggy brown hair and a cluster of pimples on the tip of his nose. If he's angry, it's hard to tell; the corners of his eyes and mouth seem to droop naturally, making him look sad more than anything.

"Sorry," I say, though I'm not sure why.

He doesn't respond. Instead he takes a silver lighter from a shoe box filled with other assorted fire starters—matchbooks, butane, twigs—and flicks it open. A small flame appears, which he holds millimeters above an unblemished spot on the piece of paper on the desk in front of him. After a few seconds, the paper bubbles toward the flame, then pops, releasing a shower of tiny orange embers.

I run for the door. Under normal circumstances I wouldn't be so quick to tattle—or maybe I would; it's hard to know now. In any case, these aren't normal circumstances. And just because I'm going to die tonight doesn't mean everyone else should.

"Annika!"

She's in the hallway, one fist raised to knock. In her other hand is a glass ashtray.

"Will you please give this to Lemon?" she yells, still smiling.

"But—"

"Thanks!" She thrusts the ashtray at me and hurries down the hall. "See you at dinner!"

Dumbfounded, I stand there and watch her leave.

Kilter Academy's other residents better be in the mood for barbecue.

Chapter 4

At 5:45 I close the comic book I've been staring at for three hours. I get up from the bed and put on my shoes. I comb my hair and part it neatly to one side, the way Mom likes. Then, not wanting to go to dinner alone—as if having company will change what's about to happen—I turn to Lemon.

The last flame fizzled out a while ago, but he's still sitting at his desk. He's slumped forward, his head resting on the closed shoe box and his arms hanging slack at his sides. I'd worry the smoke had suffocated him if his back didn't slowly lift and expand every few seconds.

Should I wake him? What if he freaks and throws fireballs at my face? Or flicks lit matches at my hair?

To be on the safe side, I head for the watercooler. I have two full cups in hand when my eyes land on a small table next to the cooler. On the table is a black cordless phone.

My heart lifts. I swap the cups for the phone, glance behind me to make sure Lemon's still out, and run to the closet. I squeeze between hanging T-shirts and sweatshirts that reek of smoke and gasoline and close the door. Unlike regular phones, this one has only one button, labeled TALK, which I press.

"It was an accident," I whisper as the other line rings. "A misunderstanding. I would never intentionally—"

"Thank you for calling the Hoodlum Hotline, how may I direct your call?"

It takes me a second to register the unfamiliar female voice. "I'm sorry. The what?"

"Hoodlum Hotline. Would you like to report a theft?"

"No."

"Stink bomb?"

"No."

"Lie?"

I pause. It's true that I killed Miss Parsippany. It's not true that I meant to. Is this what she means? Before I can ask, there's a loud banging outside the closet. Beneath me, the floorboards jump.

"I'll call you back," I say, and hang up.

"It's gonna blow!"

I fling open the door. Lemon's standing in the middle of the room. He's breathing heavily, and his eyes are wide but unfocused. The chair he'd been sitting in is lying on its side. Before I can figure out what's going on, he lunges for the watercooler and throws both arms around it.

"Stay back!" he yells. "Just stay back and no one gets hurt!"

The watercooler's wide—and heavy. When he lifts the clear globe from its base, he stumbles backward under the weight, holding the globe up so the water inside doesn't gush everywhere. He's still struggling to remain upright when I take one of the cups I'd left on the small side table and throw its contents in his face.

He stops. Blinks. Replaces the watercooler.

"Dude," he says.

"Sorry." I look at the empty cup I still hold, like it—and not me—is somehow responsible for the water dripping from his chin. "You seemed upset. I thought you were having a nightmare."

He pauses. "Was I talking?"

"You might've mentioned something about everyone staying back," I say.

His chin, still dripping, falls toward his chest. I brace for more yelling, but he just shakes his head and tousles his damp hair. He stands up straight, slides his feet into a pair of worn suede moccasins, and starts for the door.

I watch the door close. A second later it swings in again. It's propped open by a blistered, scarred hand.

I put back the phone, check my appearance once more, and scoot through the door's narrow opening. I'm so short I can pass under his arm without ducking.

"I'm Seamus, by the way." I've never held out my hand when introducing myself to someone my own age, but I do now. Lemon's likely the very last new person I'll ever meet. Commemorating the occasion with a handshake only seems fitting.

"Nice suit," he says, without returning the gesture.

I look down and remember that I changed my clothes. I'd thought Mom would want me to wear the navy-blue slacks and jacket since this, like the National Junior Honor Society induction she'd originally bought the uncomfortable clothes for, is a kind of momentous occasion, but now I feel silly. A dozen other kids fill the hallway on their way to dinner, and they're all wearing jeans, T-shirts, and sweatshirts, like it's any other day.

I'm the only one dressed for a funeral. Probably because I'm the only one about to attend one.

Lemon shuffles away. I stay a few paces behind, fiddling with my gold robot-shaped cuff links. They were a gift from Dad, whom I'd give anything to see right now.

We go outside, cross the garden, and enter the Kanteen. Kilter's dining hall is a large building with cathedral ceilings and a wall of windows that look out onto rolling lawns and distant snow-capped mountains.

"Welcome, welcome!" a familiar voice declares.

I spot Annika weaving through the crowd of kids. She's smiling, but my stomach turns anyway. As the crowd shifts right, toward a wall lined with what look like take-out windows, I turn left and follow Annika to her table. It's longer than the others and sits in the middle of the room.

"Hi," I say when I reach her.

"Seamus!" She beams. "How are you? Is everything to your liking?"

"Everything's great," I say, thinking she's kind to still care. "I was just—"

"Wait." The guy sitting next to her puts one hand on her arm. "Is this him?"

"Seamus Hinkle?" the young woman sitting on the other side of the guy says.

"*The* Seamus Hinkle?" the guy repeats, like I might be a clone.

The other adults at the table stop eating and talking. They exchange knowing looks. Some smile. Others seem to study me, probably searching for hints of a decent human being buried somewhere inside my criminal body.

I look down, my face burning hotter than Lady Lorraine's deep fryer. They know what I did. This shouldn't be surprising, but I was kind of hoping my deep, dark secret could stay between Annika and me. At least until I was no longer around to hear the gossip it started.

"Everyone," Annika says, "I'm very pleased to introduce *the* Seamus Hinkle. Our newest and most promising student."

My head snaps up.

"Seamus, I'd like you to meet your teachers. This is Harold, Fern, Wyatt, Samara, Devin, Lizzie, and Mr. Tempest."

Mr. Tempest is the only one not called by his first name. He's also the only one who seems more interested in dinner than in me. He gives me a quick once-over before returning to his cheeseburger.

"It's nice to meet you," I say. I don't know what's going on, but I do know Mom would want me to mind my manners until the bitter end.

"The pleasure's ours," Wyatt says. "Trust us."

"Don't mind them," Annika says. "They're a little excited."

"A little?" Fern chimes in.

"This is a very special occasion," Annika explains. "Normally we stop accepting applications six months before the school year starts and make our final admissions decisions three months after that. No exceptions. Yet here we are, one month into the semester . . . and we've accepted you."

"At the drop of a hat," Devin says.

"Or the throw of an apple," Lizzie adds.

They grin. I squeeze my hands into fists at my sides to keep from fanning my face. A single word forms at the base of my throat. When it reaches my mouth, my lips press tightly together as if the last meal before my *real* last meal is about to come shooting out.

I force my eyes to Annika's. They glitter in the candlelight.

"Why?" I manage.

"Because we finally had reason to make an exception." She leans toward me, lowering her voice so only I can hear. "*You*, Seamus Hinkle . . . are Kilter Academy's very first murderer."

For just a second, everything goes white. The room falls silent. I think I must be dead already—maybe from some super-fast chemical injection Annika just stuck me with, or from a heart attack so strong it killed me before I felt it—but then color slowly returns. Conversations resume.

My body was only reacting to that terrible word.

"Breakfast?" I whisper.

Annika cocks her head. Cups one hand to her ear. "What's that?"

I swallow. Try again. "Is there breakfast? Tomorrow? For me?"

Annika laughs. The teachers laugh. The only ones who don't laugh are me—and Mr. Tempest.

"Of course," she says. "Breakfast, lunch, dinner. Dessert,

midnight snacks. You may have whatever you want tomorrow, the next day, and every day after that."

I should be relieved. From the sounds of it, I'm not dying anytime soon. But I'm still reeling from the *M* word and the fact that these adults aren't.

Annika reaches over and squeezes my arm. "You've had a long day. Have some dinner and relax tonight. Everything will become clearer tomorrow."

"Right," I say, turning around. "Okay."

"Oh, and Seamus?"

I turn back. The teachers talk among themselves as Annika waves me closer. I step toward her, and she holds what looks like an oversize cell phone toward me. The small screen's filled with words. She scrolls too quickly for me to see what they say, but I can tell there are a lot of them.

"Have you ever kept a diary?" she asks quietly.

"What? No." Everyone knows diaries are for girls.

"They're very handy. If you're ever sad, or confused, or worried, and feel like you have no one to talk to, it can help to write about what you're feeling and why. At least, it always helps me."

Two questions come to mind right away. One, what makes

Annika, who can double as a military sergeant, sad or confused or worried? And two, why is she telling me this? Before I can decide whether to ask either question, she reaches for her fork.

"Enjoy your dinner," she says with a smile.

I'm still confused, but we're clearly done. So I turn around and start across the crowded dining room. The teachers' voices fade as I near the take-out windows.

"Hello there," the man behind the glass says when I reach the counter. He wears a bright red Kilter Kanteen T-shirt and baseball cap. A silver name tag reads HUGH. "Dig the threads."

"Thanks," I say.

"Got a name?"

I pause. "Seamus Hinkle."

If news of Kilter's most promising new student has reached Hugh, he doesn't show it. His expression doesn't change as he taps the thin computer screen before him. "Fish sticks. Extra crispy. Sides of mayo and honey mustard. Yes?"

I open my mouth to say yes just as the counter before me drops away. It flips upside down and rises back up with a gleaming silver tray. The tray's domed lid is so shiny I can see the beads of sweat above my shirt collar.

"Enjoy," Hugh says.

I thank him, take the tray, and scan the room for an empty seat. I spot Lemon slurping from a bowl of cereal, his eyes glued to the *South Park* episode playing on the small flat-screen attached to the back of his tray. I'd consider joining him, but all the chairs near his are taken. In fact, the only chairs that *aren't* taken are in the far right corner of the room. This isn't surprising, considering they're the only ones surrounded by bookshelves instead of TVs. Deciding a little time to myself might be nice to process everything that just happened, I head that way.

Once seated, I rest the tray on my lap and lift the lid.

"Wow," I say. I can't help it. The fish sticks are huge—five of Lady Lorraine's would equal one of these. They're golden instead of orange. And when I tap them with a fork, the crunchy coating cracks, but they don't instantly snap in half.

Impressed but still skeptical, since I've never had better than Lady Lorraine's, I break off a piece, dip it first into the mayo, then the honey mustard, and pop it into my mouth.

"Wow," I say again, though with my mouth full it sounds more like "Wha."

They're so delicious I manage to temporarily forget why I'm

here. As I clear my plate, my eyes fall on a silver button in the bottom right corner of my tray. Carved in intricate script along the base is SECONDS.

I look up and around, like someone might be watching and waiting for me to make a wrong move, to give in to temptation and ask for more than I deserve.

As it turns out, someone *is* watching. There was no one here when I sat down, but now a girl sits two chairs away. She has fair skin, a pink nose, and auburn hair that hangs down one shoulder in a loose braid. She's wearing those pants that are too short to be real pants and too long to be shorts, a baggy green sweater, and Converse sneakers. Like me, she's sitting by herself.

"What did you want?" she asks.

At least that's what I think she says. I'm too distracted by her eyes, which are reddish brown. Kind of like worn pennies.

"Sorry?" I say.

"From Annika. You went up to ask her something, right? And she started talking before you could?"

My mouth opens, but nothing comes out.

"I didn't hear what she said, if that's what you're worried about."

That's exactly what I'm worried about. And why should I believe this girl? What if she heard everything and plans to broadcast it to the whole school? But if she *did* hear everything, would she really be sitting here right now? Wouldn't she want to stay as far away from me as she could get?

She's still waiting for an answer. I look down and trace the SECONDS script with one finger as I try to come up with one.

"Laundry," I finally say. "I was going to ask if we do it ourselves, or if—"

I stop when I look up.

Because the girl's gone.

My entire body burns in embarrassment. As I reach for my water glass, my eyes fall to my jacket sleeves.

And I see that my robot cuff links are gone too.

Chapter 5

I don't want to answer any more uncomfortable questions, so I spend the rest of the night reading comic books in my room. The next thing I know, sunlight's streaming through the blinds. Drool's sliding down my chin. Lemon's standing by his desk, holding a frying pan over a flaming trash can.

Instantly awake, I sit up. Scoot back. Keep both eyes on the fire.

"Relax," Lemon says. "This one's under control."

This one? As opposed to all the others that weren't?

"Class starts in ten minutes," he adds.

"What class?" I manage.

"The schedule's on your K-Pak. Your K-Pak's on the desk."

I watch the fire for another second, then slide out of bed and take what looks like an oversize iPhone from the desk. It resembles the device Annika had at dinner last night. It turns on immediately, and the screen fills with six pulsating blue words.

SEAMUS HINKLE, YEAR ONE, SEMESTER ONE

"It can ID you by any part of your body," Lemon says.

"Like fingerprinting?" I ask, watching the blue letters fade.

He slides his K-Pak from the pocket of his jeans. He holds it out so I can see the dark screen, then places it on the floor and presses on it with one bare big toe. The surface illuminates with a glowing imprint and six pulsating blue words.

LEMON OLIVER, YEAR ONE, SEMESTER ONE

"Is Lemon your real name?" I ask.

He doesn't answer. He bends down, snatches up the device, and returns to the flaming trash can, which does appear to be under control. A bag of bread and a carton of eggs, both opened, sit on his desk.

While he cooks, I play with the mini computer. I touch a rotating envelope labeled K-MAIL, and the screen fills with a dozen or so unread messages. I open the one titled "Hinkle, S., Schedule."

"Biology?" I read. "Math? Art?" These courses don't sound any different from the ones I'd been taking at Cloudview Middle School.

As fast as my heart fell, it lifts again. Does this mean I'll be going *back* to Cloudview Middle School? And that these courses are only to make sure I don't fall too far behind?

The thought's so encouraging that I find clean jeans and a T-shirt in my duffel bag and change my clothes. I even hang up the suit in my closet to keep it from wrinkling further, just in case there's another reason to wear it later.

I'm straightening the white button-down shirt on a hanger when I remember the robot cuff links. They're still missing. I'd asked members of the Kanteen cleaning crew if they'd happened to come across them, but they hadn't. I don't know how I could've lost them either, since I'd been fiddling with them only minutes before they'd disappeared, and I'd barely moved in my chair.

Done cooking, Lemon takes the trash can to the bathroom and turns on the water. I hurry across the room, grab the phone, and hit talk.

"Hoodlum Hotline," a woman says. She sounds like the same one as yesterday.

"Hi, I'm calling to report a . . ." My voice trails off. What am I calling to report? "Um, I have—I had—these cuff links. They were a gift from my dad, and I was wearing them at dinner last night, but then they disappeared."

"Disappeared."

"Yes."

"You were looking at them one minute and then in the next—poof! They were gone? Right before your eyes?"

Realizing how this sounds, I pause. "Pretty much."

"So you think someone stole them?"

"What? No, I—"

"You're reporting a theft?"

The bathroom's silent now. Worrying that Lemon's listening, I bring the receiver closer to my mouth, cup my hand around it, and lower my voice. "I'm not sure that's what happened, I just—"

"Seamus Hinkle," the woman says loudly, as if dictating to someone else in the room with her. "Tattling in the first degree!"

There's a click, and the line goes dead.

Lemon comes back into the room with the smoking trash

can. He tosses his empty paper plate on top of its black, wet contents, grabs his backpack from the desk chair, and steps into his moccasins on his way to the door. "Later."

"Wait." I drop the phone to its base and dart around the room, gathering my sneakers and K-Pak, a notebook and pen. By the time I close and lock the door, Lemon's already rounding a corner down the hall. "I'm coming!"

He doesn't stop, but he does slow down. I catch up and together we leave the dorms and walk through the main courtyard. We don't talk, and that's fine by me, because I'm taking advantage of this time I didn't think I'd have to breathe the fresh air, listen to the birds, admire the fall colors. Were leaves always so pretty? I'll have to ask Mom the next time we speak.

"Have you talked to your parents since you got here?" I ask Lemon as we enter another building. This one has three floors. With its sleek, wooden exterior and shiny windows, it looks like some sort of futuristic ski lodge.

"Nope."

That's all we have time for before he shuffles into a classroom. I follow. When he passes the rows of desks in favor of a couch at the back of the room, I find an empty desk in the second row. I'd sit in the first row to make a good impression, but no one else is, and I don't want to stand out.

More kids enter the classroom. Most appear to be around my age, a few a year or two younger. They take their seats and unpack notebooks and pens. I wonder where they're from, what they did to get here.

According to the schedule, class should begin at nine a.m. I watch the second hand go around the clock hanging above the door. At 8:59 my pulse quickens. At 8:59 and thirty seconds, my face warms. At 8:59 and fifty-five seconds, I wipe my forehead with my T-shirt sleeve.

As the second hand nears twelve, I brace for the shrill ringing of a bell and a stern adult throwing open the door and striding into the room. That's how Mr. Carlton, my homeroom teacher back at Cloudview, starts the day, and he's in charge of a class of normal, fairly well-behaved students. Who knows how serious a teacher of troubled youth will be? What if he yells? Or gives us eight hours of homework a night? Or—

The door opens. I hold my breath, but there's no bell. There's no stern, angry adult either. There's only a tall teenager who looks like he just woke up.

"Hey," he says.

I think he'll take a seat with the rest of us, but instead he goes to the desk at the front of the room, plops into the chair, and yawns. I recognize him from Annika's introductions last night; I think his name is Harold. He's wearing faded jeans, an orange T-shirt with a white outline of two crossed, shackled fists, and aviator sunglasses. His dark blond hair hangs to his shoulders; it's tangled and knotted, like he hasn't brushed it in days.

Still wearing his sunglasses, he puts a duffel bag on the desk and reaches inside. When he pulls out a stuffed unicorn, a groan comes from the back of the room.

"How did you *do* that?" a girl asks. "I hid it so well after last class."

"Not well enough, I guess." Harold pulls his arm back and launches the unicorn forward. It lands in front of a girl with short blond hair. "Ten demerits for Houdini, zero for the Gabster."

Next he pulls out a comic book.

"*Betty and Veronica Double Digest*? I don't even know if I should give this back." But with one flick of the wrist, he sends it flying through the air. It lands on the desk of a kid with spiky black hair, who picks it up and smacks his forehead with it. "Another ten demerits for the master magician. Zilch for Abe."

He pulls an iPod, key chain, and sweater from the bag. A Frisbee, Slinky, and jump rope. A long lighter shaped like a matchstick goes to Lemon. Kids smile and frown, happy to have their things back but annoyed they lost them in the first place. I'm trying to figure out what's going on when Harold, who apparently likes to be called Houdini, pulls out a green satin ribbon. He pinches one end of the ribbon between his pointer finger and thumb and holds it in front of him.

"Elinor, Elinor."

He shakes his head. I turn in my chair to watch the girl with the red hair and warm copper eyes walk to the front of the room.

"Not nearly as challenging as I'd hoped," Houdini says when she reaches him.

She takes the ribbon and starts back for her seat. As she nears my row I offer a small, encouraging smile, but she doesn't see it. She simply looks straight ahead and ties back her hair in a perfect green bow.

Houdini claps his hands together. I jump. Turning back, I see that he's pushed his sunglasses on top of his head . . . and is looking straight at me.

"*Hola*, Hinkle," he says with a grin.

I look behind me, like I really do have a clone following my every move.

"New kid's confused. Anyone care to explain what just happened?"

My classmates turn and check me out. I slide down in my chair.

"Nobody wants to take the gold star hit, huh?" Houdini asks. "Fair enough. I'll—"

"Houdini stole our stuff."

I look behind me again. This time, Elinor's looking back.

"For class," she says. "Every week he tries to take something of ours without us knowing. When he succeeds, he gets demerits. When he doesn't, we do."

New kid's even more confused now.

"But I thought this was math," I say.

"It is," Elinor says. "At Kilter, math is the addition and subtraction of personal belongings."

"Heads up."

I look at Houdini just in time to see him chuck two small, shiny objects my way.

"Kilter Academy Rule Number One," he says. "Don't dress to impress. You have more important things to worry about than whether your socks match your shoes—or your cuff links match your stuffy button-down shirt, as the case may be."

Heart racing, I grab the gold robots and shove them into my jeans pocket.

"Who wants to share Rule Number Two?" Houdini asks.

There's a long pause. Then Elinor says, "Get as many demerits and as few gold stars as possible. That's how we're graded here. Demerits are like As and gold stars are like Fs."

What about Bs and Cs? Isn't there something between demerits and gold stars? Like gray triangles?

And in what weird academic world are demerits considered a *good* thing?

"Rule Number Three?" Houdini prompts.

"You have to go to classes," Elinor continues. "We have six a day, Monday through Friday. Three in the morning and three in the afternoon. Every now and then we have a special history lecture, which we find out about from K-Mail. When you're not in class, you should be completing assignments, studying, and having fun."

"You have thousands of complimentary items at your disposal," Houdini adds. "TVs, movies, video games, you name it. Just press the party hat icon on your K-Pak and order from the long list of fun items that appears. And speaking of fun, Rule Number Four?"

"You have to get all your teachers," Elinor says.

"Get?" I ask, heart racing. "What does that mean?"

Houdini explains. "Kilter faculty members, including yours truly, will teach you specific skills useful in surprising, scaring, or otherwise messing with adults. In order to advance to the next training level, by the end of the semester you must use these skills to surprise, scare, or otherwise mess with your teachers. You can do so anytime, anyplace. The only restriction is that you get each instructor with the skills they teach."

"So to get you," I say slowly, trying to put it together, "I'd have to steal something of yours?"

"Without me knowing." Houdini grins. "Good luck with that. I'm almost as tough as Mr. Tempest."

Mr. Tempest. He was the older teacher at Annika's dinner table last night. "What does he do?" I ask.

"He's the school historian. He hardly ever leaves Annika's

side, so he's very hard to get. In fact, he's the only faculty member you can get by any means necessary—and who you don't *have* to get in order to advance."

"That doesn't mean you can't try," a kid calls out from across the room.

"But it does mean you probably won't succeed. If for some strange reason you do, you'll receive extra credit—and much respect from the entire Kilter community." Houdini nods to Elinor. "Last rule?"

"There are no other rules," Elinor says.

"Any questions?" Houdini asks.

"Yeah," says a kid at the back of the room. "We already know all this, *and* we're supposed to learn how to swipe candy from store register racks today. Why are we wasting so much time on the new guy?"

Houdini shoots him a look. "Because—"

"I have a question."

Houdini forgets about the kid at the back of the room and grins at me. "Awesome. Give it up, Hinkle."

I just wanted to stop him from telling everyone what Annika told me last night—that I'm Kilter's first murderer—and now I

try to pick from the millions of questions spinning through my head.

"Can we talk to our parents?"

The class bursts into groans and giggles. Clearly, this was the wrong choice.

"Sure," Houdini says. "But who here really wants to?"

I raise my hand. When there are more giggles, I look behind me and see that I'm the only one. So I lower it.

"No worries, Hinkle. I get it. Your parents think they've signed you up for a kick-butt reform school, and you think they should know that's not the case. But I guarantee that if you give Kilter some time, you'll have no desire to share our little secret. And if ever you're tempted to spill the beans, just remember whose idea it was for you to come here." Houdini tilts back in his chair, rests his feet on the desk. "Who are your parents going to believe? The adults they've entrusted to mold you into a model citizen? Or the terrible kid they're so desperate to control?"

He gives this a moment to sink in. Knowing it'll take much longer than that, I quickly ask my next question.

"But if this isn't a reform school . . . what is it?"

Houdini's feet drop to the floor. He leans forward. Holds my

eyes with his. "A world-renowned, top secret training facility."

I want to look away but can't.

"Kilter Academy for Troubled Youth doesn't accept just anyone," Houdini continues. "Each semester, the admissions board receives thousands of applications and fills only thirty slots. Acceptance is based on a number of criteria, the most important being a student's natural talent for bad behavior."

"Like the kind we get grounded for?" I ask.

"Exactly."

"But we're not here to learn good behavior?"

"Nope."

I try to solve this puzzle on my own, but it makes no sense. "Then what exactly are we training for?"

Houdini's grin takes up his whole face and makes him look even younger than he is.

"You're training," he says, "to become professional Trouble-makers."

Chapter 6

After class, Houdini asks for volunteers to show me something called the Kommissary. When no one jumps at the chance, I volunteer to show myself. After all, the more time I spend alone, the fewer questions I'll have to answer. But then Houdini throws a piece of chalk at Lemon, snapping him out of a midsnooze snore, and says that unless Lemon wants to die alone in a blaze of nonglory, he'll do everything he can to be the best roommate anyone's ever had.

Personally, I think being a good roommate includes making

conversation, but Lemon doesn't seem to agree. We walk silently until I finally ask the question I've been thinking since Houdini told me what we're training to become.

"So, what's a professional Troublemaker, anyway?"

Lemon doesn't answer. He doesn't even blink.

"I mean, I know what a normal troublemaker is," I say, thinking of Bartholomew John. "At least, I think I do. But what's the difference between that and a professional? Do we get paid or something?"

"Does it really matter? Making trouble's fun. Just go with it."

Just go with it. Right. No problem.

"By the way," Lemon says a moment later, "you're the thirteenth."

"The thirteenth what?" I ask.

"Roommate."

"Cool." Then, "But you've only been here a month, right?"

Silence.

"So that would be, what? Three roommates a week?" I ask.

"One week, twelve roommates. Nine first-year Troublemakers like us, and one second-year, one third-year, and one fourth-year. They couldn't deal with my little fire hobby, and the housing department couldn't find anyone else to bunk with me. Until yesterday, I'd been by myself for twenty-one days."

My heart sinks. "Sorry. Having your own room must've been nice."

He shrugs. "I'll have it again soon. Unless they're right about you."

"What do you mean?" I struggle to keep my voice casual.

"I mean, I don't know what your deal is." He stops before a glass door. Faces me. Lifts one furry eyebrow. "But I do know they wouldn't have paired you with me if they didn't think you could handle the heat."

He goes inside. I wait for the feeling to return to my feet before following him.

"Welcome to the Kommissary! Please place one hand on the print pad."

There's a silver turnstile just inside the entrance. Next to it is a clear podium topped with a thin, clear box. A long counter is to the right of the podium, behind which an older Kilter employee smiles at me. According to the tag on his red shirt, his name's Martin.

"The print pad?" Martin repeats. "Can't get in without it?"

My eyes follow his nod to the clear box. My chest tightens. I don't want to leave and annoy Lemon by wasting his time, but I also don't want to set off alarms, alert security—or, worst of all, prompt confetti to fall from the ceiling and a marching band to escort me inside. Given Annika's high opinion of murderers, this type of celebration is a real possibility.

"Because wasting an hour of valuable class time wasn't enough?"

I spin around. The kid with spiky black hair is behind me. The girl whose stuffed unicorn Houdini stole is behind him. Four older Troublemakers are behind her. They all look at me expectantly.

"Sorry," I say. "I've never been here before."

"We heard." The kid—Abe, I think Houdini called him—rolls his eyes. "It's not rocket science. Put your hand on the pad and wait for the turnstile to beep."

I consider letting him go first and trying to scoot through the turnstile as he passes through, but Martin's watching us. And Troublemaker after Troublemaker joins the line until it's out the door. With no time to figure out how to buy more time, I turn back, close my eyes . . . and place my right palm on the clear box.

The box moves. My eyes snap open. I try to move my hand, but a force keeps my fingers attached, as if they're magnets and the box is a refrigerator. The box, which I now see is a computer screen, tilts to a forty-five-degree angle and stops. Words scroll across the screen just above my fingertips.

WELCOME, SEAMUS HINKLE! YOU HAVE . . . −20 CREDITS!

Abe snorts. Unicorn girl giggles. Martin says, "Everyone starts somewhere. And if rumors are right, soon you'll be buying the Kilter Über-Airkraft."

The snorts and giggles stop.

"The Kilter Über-Airkraft costs fifty thousand credits," Abe says. "It's the most expensive thing the Kommissary sells."

"I know," Martin says, and winks at me.

The turnstile beeps. I burst through, nearly taking down the display of drinking straws and spitball glue on the other side.

Eager to get away from my classmates, I dart down the first aisle I come to. It's filled with every kind of ammunition a Troublemaker could want, like BB guns and paintball rifles. Bows and arrows. Water Uzis and ice-pellet pistols. Balloons that look like ones you'd blow up for a birthday party, but whose name—Hydra-Bomb—suggests a much more sinister purpose.

My weapon was nothing like these, but they still make me think of Miss Parsippany. I look straight ahead until I'm past the section.

After checking the other aisles, I finally find Lemon at the back of the store. He stands before a wall of supplies labeled A FIREFIGHTER'S WORST NIGHTMARE. As I get closer I see that this nightmare consists of matchbooks and lighters. Packs of kindling and shredded newspaper. Aerosol gasoline cans. Heatproof masks and bodysuits.

And the thing that Lemon's staring at like it's a swinging pendulum: the Kilter Smoke Detector with Automatic Flame Eliminator. The perforated silver disc is in a glass case at the top of the wall, near the ceiling.

"Are you going to buy that?" I ask.

"It's two thousand credits," he says.

"How many do you have?"

His head turns toward me. His eyes narrow.

"I have negative twenty," I offer.

He doesn't smile, but his eyes return to their normal half-lidded position.

"How do I get more?" I ask, not wanting him to think I'm some sort of nosy busybody.

He looks up again. "You automatically get ten a week. Like an allowance, only you don't have to make your bed for it. The rest you get by making trouble, either through completing assignments or on your own, and earning demerits. One demerit gets you one credit."

"Do gold stars get you anything?"

"Yes. Credits taken away." His eyes shift toward me. "You must've done something really right—as in wrong—in the short time you've been here to be in the red zone. Like maybe calling the Hoodlum Hotline?"

My heart stops. "That gets you gold stars?"

"And alerts Kilter security. That's why Troublemakers sometimes take the hit. Ratting out the competition can lead to the competition being stopped, which is worth losing a few credits every now and then."

I'm still trying to process this as Lemon's eyes shift back and he continues.

"Your K-Pak has something called the Kilter Report Kard, which updates your demerit and gold star totals every hour. The icon's on the main screen. It's a red apple."

Of course it is.

"Do you lose demerits as you use credits?" I ask.

"No. Annika doesn't want your shopping habits to make you forget how much trouble you're actually making. So the number of demerits and gold stars will only go up the longer you're here. Your credits, though, will go up and down. To check them, press the dollar-sign icon on your K-Pak." He reaches forward and takes a book of matches from the wall. "If you want to catch up fast, go after our teachers, like, now."

An image of Miss Parsippany falling to the floor flashes before my eyes. I shake my head. It goes away.

"You heard Houdini," he says. "You have to at some point. And you get a hundred demerits for each one, so if you want to make up for lost time, you should start big."

"What if I can't get them? Or earn any demerits, for that matter?" Because before the Unfortunate Apple Incident, I didn't get into trouble. And I'm pretty sure I'll fail every assignment here.

"Then—"

"Lemonade!"

Lemon steps away from the wall. Turns. Slides his hands into his jeans pockets. "Abraham."

The kid with the spiky black hair saunters up. He has a case of spray paint under one arm and a lollipop in his mouth. "What's cooking? Or maybe the better question is—what's *not* cooking?"

Lemon doesn't answer. I feel like I should defend him from something, but I'm not sure what.

"Still fantasizing about the Kilter Smoke Detector with Automatic Flame Eliminator?" Abe slurps on his lollipop. "Too bad demerits don't come with coupons."

"Heads up," Gabby, the unicorn girl says, joining us. "Fern's here—and she's in rubber-ball oblivion."

Gabby lifts her chin. We follow it to a pyramid of rubber balls. They come in every color of the rainbow and are arranged by size. The kind you can sit and bounce around on are at the base, their handles pointed down. The kind you can get for a quarter from those old gumball machines are at the top. In between are soccer balls, basketballs, and other balls I've never seen before.

Next to the pyramid is a young woman with dark curly hair that stands around her head like she just stuck her fingers in an electrical outlet. She wears white glasses that point up at the corners. I recognize her from Annika's introductions last night. As we watch, she takes a ball from the top of the display, holds it near her ear, and shakes it.

Lemon nudges me. "Now's your chance."

"For what?"

"Getting out of the red. Make her laugh, cry, pass out, whatever."

"How?" I ask.

"Fern's the gym teacher," Gabby explains. "Dodgeball's her specialty. Which means—"

"I have to throw balls at her?" I finish.

"Exactly." Gabby smiles, like this is her idea of a good time.

"No way," I say. "Not going to happen."

"Awesome." Abe snorts, then moves the lollipop to one side of his mouth until his left cheek bulges. "Stand your ground. You'll really get ahead that way."

Lemon shoots him a look before stepping toward me. "This is as easy as it gets. She's distracted. The place is crawling with kids. There's no way she'll know who did it."

Maybe she won't. But *I* will.

"If it's such an easy shot, why don't you guys take it?" I ask. "You've been here longer. You deserve it more than I do."

"I got her last week," Gabby says.

"Two weeks ago," Lemon says.

"Our first day," Abe says, then cracks the lollipop between his teeth.

I try to think of another excuse but can't. Fern does seem much more interested in the rubber pyramid than in anyone around it . . . but what if she's just pretending to be distracted so that some naive Troublemaker makes a move? And is immediately caught?

"What's the matter?" Abe asks. "Never messed with someone twice your size before?"

A series of images flashes through my head: Bartholomew John's crooked grin. Fish sticks doused in milk. Apples flying through the air. Miss Parsippany falling to the ground.

I look at Abe, then nod at Lemon. "Be right back."

They huddle together as I make my way toward the rubber pyramid. When Fern replaces one ball and circles the display for another, I duck behind a shelf of microwavable tar and feathers. She looks up once, and I think our eyes meet—which makes my pulse hammer so loudly in my ears I can't hear anything else—but then she simply takes a softball from the pyramid and gives it a squeeze.

My heart still racing, I scan my surroundings for something

to throw. Tar and feathers are out of the question. So are pocket flashlights and night-vision goggles. Only one other display is within arm's reach: Hydra-Bombs. They're made of rubber, and the samples, which are filled with water, resemble balls more than they do balloons . . . but I'm still not sure they'll count. I could check the rest of the store for the real deal, but I know I'll chicken out as soon as the rubber pyramid's out of sight. And if I try to snatch one from the pyramid itself, I risk being seen by Fern.

Hydra-Bombs it is.

There are three on a glass shelf. I take the smallest one, which is the size of a tennis ball. The rubber's somehow soft and firm at the same time. According to the illustration below the shelf, even the smallest model is powerful enough to shatter a glass window from twenty feet away.

But I won't shatter anything. Not this time.

Still behind the tar-and-feathers display, I face forward and watch Fern. She might be the slowest shopper I've ever seen. She taps, squeezes, and shakes each option. Holds one ball in each hand and lifts and lowers both. Shines them on her jacket and inspects the result. Mom tests fruit the same way at the grocery store, but in about a tenth of the time.

She takes so long I start to lose my nerve. Who cares if I stay in the red? So what if I never earn another demerit? Is making a good impression here more important than making sure what happened to Miss Parsippany never happens again?

It's not. So I turn back. Reach forward to replace the Hydra-Bomb.

"Chicken," Abe scoffs nearby. "I could tell just by looking at him."

Calcium. It helps you grow.

And turn around again.

I'll miss. I'll throw . . . and I'll miss. Looking like I tried has to be worth something.

On the wall behind Fern is a poster of a smiling kid wearing head-to-toe Kilter attire: a gray baseball hat, sweatshirt, and sweatpants, all bearing the silver KA logo. He has blond hair and chubby cheeks, and if I don't look too closely, he resembles Bartholomew John. His face will make a perfect target.

I hold my breath. Pull back my arm. Imagine the high, invisible arc the Hydra-Bomb will make as it sails near—but over—Fern's head. I start to bring my arm forward and open my fingers—

—just as someone rams into me. The Hydra-Bomb flies from my hand, and I fall to the ground.

But not before I see the water balloon hit a basketball in the center of the rubber pyramid. The pyramid explodes. Dozens of balls shoot through the air. Four of them hit Fern—in her shoulder, chest, stomach, and rear end, rotating her like a machine gun does a soldier on a video-game battlefield. As she falls to the floor, her lips form a perfect, surprised O.

"Sorry, man!"

My eyes are closed. I open them to see an older Troublemaker standing over me. He tucks a remote-control airplane under his arm and holds out one hand.

"New model. Kind of got away from me. You all right?"

I take his hand and sit up. Through the legs of the tar-and-feathers display table, I see Fern climb to her knees, rub her eyes, and sift through the bouncing balls for her glasses. I'm debating whether to crawl over and help her look when she finds them and puts them on.

This time, our eyes really do meet.

"Seamus!" She beams, slaps her palms to her thighs. "I should've known."

It was an accident. I open my mouth to explain, but before I can, my book bag buzzes on my back. I slide it around, open it, and take out my K-Pak. Its screen glows red as a new K-Mail message loads.

CONGRATULATIONS, SEAMUS HINKLE! AFTER DEFEATING FERN NOOGAN, YOU'RE 100 DEMERITS CLOSER TO BEING A PROFESSIONAL TROUBLEMAKER!

Chapter 7

DEMERITS: 100
GOLD STARS: 20

Whenever Dad's confused, like when Mom disguises tofu as chicken for dinner, or when our DVD player spits out discs in the middle of movies, or when we change the clocks for daylight savings, he always says the same thing: "I don't know whether to add or subtract!" This is like other people saying they don't know which way's up or down, but Dad's an accountant, so his compass is math. Adding, subtracting, multiplying, and dividing are his north, south, east, and west.

In our room later that night, I don't know whether to add or subtract. On the one hand, in addition to a hundred demerits, successfully attacking Fern seemed to earn me cautious acceptance from my fellow first-year Troublemakers. When I rejoined them, Lemon actually smiled, Gabby patted me on the back, and Abe didn't roll his eyes once. Since I don't want to make a bad situation worse by having enemies, this is a positive development.

On the other hand, I *hit* a *teacher.* Knocked her straight to the ground. I know students are expected to do things like that here, but after what I did to Miss Parsippany, it just feels wrong.

Which raises a very important question.

"Why?"

Lemon lies in bed with his back to me, making shadow puppets on the wall with one hand and a butane lighter. My question is followed by a click. The small flame goes out.

"Why what?"

I've been staring at the same page in my comic book for an hour. Now I sit up and toss it to the end of the bed.

"Why are we here?"

"Because we did bad things at home? And our parents didn't know what else to do with us?"

That part I get. "But why a school for Troublemakers? What

are we supposed to do with our new skills when we leave? What's the point?"

Lemon doesn't answer. I'm worrying I asked too many questions when he rolls over. Slowly. His left leg slides off his right leg and falls to the mattress. His body tilts, inch by inch, until gravity takes over and his back hits the bed. He recovers from the exertion for a second, then inhales deeply and rises up on his left side.

"*Hamlet*," he says.

Not wanting to press my luck, I try to crack this code on my own. But I can't.

"Sorry?" I say.

"The play. About the prince who goes after his uncle for killing his dad. By that famous dead guy."

"Shakespeare. I know, I've read it. I just don't get what that has to do with this."

"'The lady doth protest too much, methinks,'" Lemon says. "'To thine own self be true.'"

I remember those lines . . . but I still don't get it.

"The thing was written, like, a million years ago," Lemon continues. "It uses words no one has in centuries. But we still have to read it."

"So?"

"So what are we supposed to do with our new translation skills after we've finished it? What's the point in reading a story that has nothing to do with anything today?"

I open my mouth to explain that despite the archaic language, the play's themes of love and revenge are universal, eternal (or so my English teacher said last year), but then I close it. Because I think I understand.

"Our regular schools teach us stuff that's not exactly useful in the real world," I say. "Right?"

"Right. At least here we can do what we want when we want. I don't know about you, but back home I was on permanent lockdown. No friends, no movies, no fun. Compared to that, this is vacation."

I think about this. The only vacation my family ever took was to Niagara Falls, where Mom caught a bad cold after getting drenched on a boat ride and we spent the rest of the week watching *Wheel of Fortune* reruns in our tiny motel room. Even compared to that, having unlimited fish sticks, 3-D movies, and no curfew doesn't seem so bad.

Only *bad* is what I deserve. And this, I realize, is my bigger problem. After what I did, I'm lucky just to be alive. It's not right to have any fun on top of that.

But I can't talk about this to Lemon. At least not so directly.

"What about your parents?" I ask. "Don't you feel guilty that they think you're here to learn how to behave?"

His sad brown eyes meet mine, then droop shut. His body tilts toward the wall. Gravity takes over. He lies on his back, unmoving.

Now I've definitely asked too many questions.

By my pillow, my K-Pak buzzes. I reach over and open the new K-Mail message.

TO: shinkle@kilteracademy.org
FROM: annika@kilteracademy.org
SUBJECT: Kudos!

Dear Seamus,

Just a quick note to say hello and congratulate you on your successful performance in the Kommissary today. I've never seen Fern caught so off guard.

Your Kilter career is off to an impressive start. I can't wait to see where it goes from here.

Warmly,

Annika

P.S. If you need anything, anything at all, please don't hesitate to ask!

Add or subtract? Subtract or add? Once again, I'm confused. I don't know whether to be happy that Annika's pleased, or sad about what I did to make her feel that way.

I'm about to reread the note, just in case it contains clues I'm somehow missing, when my K-Pak buzzes with a new message.

TO: shinkle@kilteracademy.org
FROM: kommissary@kilteracademy.org
SUBJECT: You Got a Teacher. . . . Now Get Shopping!

Hey, Seamus!

Way to go! You earned 100 demerits for making Fern Noogan's head spin. After deducting 20 gold stars, which you got for calling the Hoodlum Hotline, that leaves you with . . . 80 credits!

The good news? You can now do a lot of damage

> at the Kommissary. The bad news? You'll have to hurry—at least if you want to snag one of our newest, hottest items. The supercool, limited edition K-Shot, called "the best introductory weapon of its kind . . . EVER" by *Trouble 'n' More* magazine, won't last long!

This is followed by an image of a small flashing camera. I press it, and a photo of a kid holding a slingshot appears. At least, I think it's a slingshot. It's shaped like a K instead of a Y, and the kid holds it horizontally instead of vertically, but the rubber band and small ball look like others I've seen in movies.

> The K-Shot can be yours for the bargain price of 75 credits. So don't wait! Pick yours up today!
>
> At Your Service,
>
> The Kommissary Krew

I start to delete the e-mail. I don't know what the Kommissary sells that I'd actually want to buy, but I do know that a weapon—a real one, unlike the one I used in the Cloudview cafeteria—isn't it. But just as I'm about to press the digital trash can, I have an idea. It might be the best one I've ever had, mostly because I know it'll help me feel better. If I hadn't been so overwhelmed by not dying, going to class, and making trouble, I would've thought of it sooner.

Kilter K-Mail looks just like my e-mail at home. There's an in-box, a sent box, and a spam box. When you start a new message, there are empty bars to type in the recipient's e-mail address and the subject. Below those is a big white square for your message.

Mom never checks her e-mail, but Dad's on his all the time for work.

I start typing.

TO: taxmannumerouno@taxmannumerouno.com
FROM: shinkle@kilteracademy.org
SUBJECT: HI!!!!

Dear Dad,

Hi! How are you?? How's Mom?? Did you guys make it home okay? What's new? How's my room?

> Everything's great here! The food's amazing, and the kids are nice. I had my first few classes today. One of them was math, which made me think of you.

I stop typing. I'm tempted to explain how math here isn't like regular math, but then I remember what Houdini said about telling our parents the truth about Kilter. Dad might believe me, but I know he'd talk to Mom before writing me back. And since it was her idea to send me away, I'm not so sure *she'd* believe me. If I try to convince her that Kilter's a top secret troublemaking training camp, she'll probably think I'm lying just so they feel bad, come pick me up, and take me home. And while murder is definitely the worst thing a kid can do, in Mom's opinion, lying isn't far behind.

No, it's best to keep it simple. At least for now.

I continue typing.

> Anyway, I have lots of homework I should get to. But I just wanted to say hi and let you know that you can e-mail me here ANYTIME. Every student gets a handheld computer that buzzes whenever a new

> message comes in. So the second your note reaches me, I'll know and write you back! Cool, huh?

I stop typing again. Now I'm tempted to apologize for what I did because, at the very least, I don't want my parents to think I've forgotten. But they know that, don't they? Wouldn't they rather read a cheery, upbeat note that suggests I'm adjusting well here? So that they'll be certain I'm all reformed and ready to leave when the time comes?

Deciding that yes, they would, I end the message as happily as I started it.

> Miss you! Love you! Hugs to Mom!
> Seamus

I check the note for typos, then hit send. I feel better immediately. After all, in the long run, it won't matter whether I add or subtract now. What *will* matter is whether my parents eventually forgive me and love me as much as they did before I became a criminal. Staying in touch while we're separated can only bring us closer to that goal.

I look over at Lemon. He couldn't have been too mad that I asked about his parents—because he fell asleep while I was writing Dad. As he snores, I retrieve my comic book from the foot of the bed. I've just turned the cover when the mattress vibrates beneath me.

I drop the comic book and lunge for my K-Pak.

Dad must be working late. He's working late, had his e-mail up, and was so happy to hear from me he wrote back right away.

An electronic message has never taken longer to load. Still, I can't stop smiling as I stare at the small screen.

Until the words appear.

> ERROR!
>
> The message you just sent, subject: "HI!!!!," to TAXMANNUMEROUNO@TAXMANNUMEROUNO.COM, is UNDELIVERABLE. Recipient's address is invalid. Please note: K-Mail is an intracampus messaging system ONLY. Messages will not reach external e-mail systems.
>
> Please also note: This is an automated response.

All replies will remain unread in an unattended in-box.
Thank you for using K-Mail!
—Your Kilter IT Department

I flop back on the bed. Pull the blanket over my head. Try to tell myself that if not talking to my parents for a few weeks is my worst punishment, then I'm the luckiest murderer who's ever lived to experience the consequences of his actions.

This might be true. But it doesn't stop my eyes from watering.

I lie like this for 127 of Lemon's snores, which I listen to in hopes that they become shorter, maybe even stop. Lemon and I aren't exactly best friends, but right now it'd be nice to have someone to talk to—about anything. When the snores only grow longer, I feel more alone than I have since coming to Kilter.

Then I remember something Annika said at dinner last night. I still don't think I'm the diary-keeping type . . . but maybe there's something to writing down the things you'd say to a friend if you had one. Deciding it can't hurt, I slide one hand out from under the blanket and feel around the mattress for my K-Pak. When my fingers curl around the cool plastic, I slide it under the covers, turn it on, and start typing.

TO: parsippany@cloudviewschools.net
FROM: shinkle@kilteracademy.org
SUBJECT: Sorry

Dear Miss Parsippany,

I did something today I didn't want to do. Something I swore I'd never do again after that day in the Cloudview cafeteria.

I hit a teacher. Not once, twice, or even three times. FOUR times. To be accurate, four rubber balls hit her, but still. I launched the attack, so it might as well have been my fists that knocked her down.

After what I did to you, I never wanted to do anything bad again. I told myself that if I just happened to do something bad again, or at least something I might get grounded for, there was no way it was going to involve another teacher. And if, for some reason, I ended up doing something bad that involved another teacher, I definitely wasn't going to do it so soon after the Unfortunate Apple Incident. That's not just bad manners; it's evil.

Well, guess what? I did something bad. To a teacher. Less than two weeks after the UAI. When I'm supposed to be at the best reform school in the country, learning how to act like a good kid.

I'd apologize to the teacher I hit, but something tells me she wouldn't want to hear it. I'd apologize to my parents for misbehaving once again, but I can't reach them. So I'm apologizing to you. After all, you deserve to hear "I'm sorry" more than anyone. And I know it's way too little, way too late . . . but that's still better than nothing, right?

In any case, I AM sorry, Miss Parsippany. For everything.

Sincerely,

Seamus Hinkle

Chapter 8

DEMERITS: 100
GOLD STARS: 35

It takes me a long time to fall asleep. My mind races like our TiVo back home does at seven o'clock each night, when Mom catches up on her recorded soap operas by skipping ahead to the yelling, crying, and kissing parts. Only instead of actors yelling, crying, and kissing, I see Houdini yawning. Balls flying. Fern beaming. Eventually, my mind jumps to an image of Elinor staring out the window in math class, and lingers there.

That's the last thing I remember before I'm wakened by screams.

"Stop!"

I shoot up in bed.

"Drop!"

Rub my eyes.

"Roll!"

Start choking.

I can just make out Lemon through the thick gray smoke. He's standing over an open suitcase filled with ash and flames.

"Stop!" he shouts again.

I hit the floor and roll before he can tell me to. Each rotation brings a sight even scarier than the one before, like Lemon closing his eyes, rocking back and forth, lighting and dropping another match. The fire grows bigger, blocking my route to the water-cooler on the other side. Smoke scalds my nose and throat, but I manage to hold my breath until I reach the phone.

"Hoodlum Hotline, how—"

"Fire," I gasp. "Flames. Big ones."

That's all I get out before the smoke hits my lungs. I start coughing and can't stop. Lemon's only a few feet away and I want to reach forward, to grab him and shake him awake, but my arms won't move. Neither will my legs. It's so hot my skin must be melting, drooping, melding me to the floor. I realize I'm still clutching the phone and force the mouthpiece before my burning lips.

"Please," I whisper. "My parents. Tell them I—"

The door swings open. Three men in matching khaki pants, plaid shirts, and red fanny packs enter the room. They move purposefully but not particularly quickly, like they've done this before. The first man takes a skinny silver tank that hangs from one of his belt loops and aims it at the fire; there's a blast of white foam, and the flames disappear. The second takes a silver box from his fanny pack, presses a button, and holds the box in one palm as it sucks up the smoke. The third opens the windows, then flicks Lemon's ear, snapping the would-be arsonist out of his slumber.

For a second, it's silent. And I'm not sure if I'm alive or dead.

"Still there?" the operator barks from the receiver on my chest.

"I think so," I croak, not bothering to lift the phone.

"Seamus Hinkle, tattling in the second degree!"

I don't realize she's hung up until the receiver starts beeping and the men turn toward me. I'm trying to still my shaking hands long enough to turn off the phone when a mask clamps over my mouth.

"Hey! What—"

"Stop talking," a low voice commands. "Breathe normally."

I don't argue. I can't. Not only are my lips locked in place, one of our rescuers presses one hand on my head to keep me from moving. He's surprisingly strong for a guy who looks like his idea of living on the edge is wearing penny loafers without socks.

I force myself to inhale and exhale. Lemon, now fully awake, also wears a mask and takes deep breaths. Seconds later, the burning in my lungs, nose, and throat fades, and Mister Rogers releases my head and mouth.

"Anyone care to share what just happened here?" the first man asks. He removes a K-Pak from his fanny pack. GS 7 runs along the miniature computer's side like a digital marquee.

I glance at Lemon. He's still standing by the smoldering suitcase, staring at the embers like he's not sure how they got there.

"We were sleeping," I explain, thinking we're about to get into big trouble. "Lemon—he was totally out. He didn't know what he was doing." When GS 7 continues to look at me without blinking, I add, "It was an accident."

GS 7 waits, like he's giving me the chance to take back what I just said. I look at Lemon. He looks at me, then turns to GS 7.

"It wasn't an accident," he says. "Sleepwalking fire-starting. It's still in the testing phase."

GS 7 lets out a low whistle. "Impressive. You'll definitely get a few demerits for that one."

"But we have to dock you two days of troublemaking," one of the other men adds.

"Fair enough," Lemon says.

With that, the men leave. Lemon goes into the bathroom and closes the door. A second later the shower turns on. The room's still light without the fire burning, and I realize it's morning. According to my K-Pak, it's 8:20—and we have a special assembly in ten minutes.

There's a common restroom down the hall. I go there to wash up and get dressed. By the time I'm back, Lemon's out of the shower and sitting on his bed. I have a million questions—like who are the GS? What do they do besides put out fires? Why was Lemon docked two days of troublemaking? Why was this announced like it's a bad thing?

And the biggest puzzle of all: Why did Lemon say the fire wasn't an accident? Why did he lie?

But my roommate's not in the mood for conversation. He

looks straight ahead when I come in. Water drips from his wet hair and slides down his nose. I offer him a dry towel; he ignores it.

He must be mad that I panicked and called the Hoodlum Hotline. I open my mouth to apologize, but before I can get out the first word, he speaks.

"How are you?"

My mouth closes. No one's asked me that since before the Unfortunate Apple Incident, when how I was became instantly and forever irrelevant. The question's so unexpected I don't know how to respond.

"Are you okay?" He still looks straight ahead, but his fingers tighten around his knees. "The fire. Did it—are you . . . ?"

Figuring out what he's trying to ask, I quickly reassure him. "I'm fine. My throat's a little dry from the smoke, but besides that, I'm totally fine."

His head drops. His fingers relax.

"Want to go see what's so special about this special assembly?" I ask.

"Yes." He releases a deep breath. "I'd like that."

We don't talk as we walk to the Performance Pavilion. I don't mind the silence, because it gives me time to process what just

happened. In fact, I'm so busy replaying the events and guessing at the answers to my own questions that I don't realize we've reached the pavilion until someone thrusts a bucket of popcorn at me.

"Butter? Salt? Caramel sauce?"

Hugh, the older employee from the Kanteen, smiles and holds up a pitcher of steaming yellow liquid. Next to him is a silver cart covered in bowls of caramel and hot fudge, and jars of salt, pepper, and other seasonings. Behind him is a five-foot-tall popper filled with swirling kernels.

"No thanks," I say.

"All of the above," Lemon says.

As Hugh douses Lemon's popcorn, I look around. We're standing on a silver carpet that leads to a gleaming steel-and-glass stadium rimmed in silver Kilter Academy flags. Besides the popcorn stand there's an ice cream hut, a hot dog station, and a candy bar featuring, among other treats, M&M's in every color of the rainbow—if rainbows had a hundred stripes instead of six and featured shades Crayola hadn't even imagined. Both sides of the carpet are lined with bunches of silver balloons. Lit sparklers are stuck in the ground between the balloon bunches, making the carpet glitter.

Dozens of kids mill about, but I recognize only a few of them from classes. The others are older and talk and laugh with the kind of ease that suggests they've been here before. They wear shiny silver ski parkas that are identical except for the KA patches on their sleeves; these are different colors and feature a variety of emblems, like a hand grenade, an outline of the human body, or smiling and frowning drama masks.

"Please take your seats!" a male voice booms from overhead speakers. "The program's about to begin!"

Kids abandon food stands and shuffle toward the entrance. I wait for Lemon to grab napkins and a soda, and then we join the crowd.

"Returning students, report to your assigned sections," the overhead voice declares. "New students, come forward!"

"Front-row seats," Lemon says. "Nice."

Mom's big on culture and has dragged Dad and me to many string-quartet performances and dance recitals at the Cloudview Community Center, so I know that to some people, mostly those with gray hair and failing vision and/or hearing, front-row seats are the best. They're the ones you pay more for or show up hours early to get. But personally? I'm not a fan. Mostly because it's a lot harder to doze off when the performers are three feet away and can see when your eyes are closed.

The pavilion, which has an enormous stage but fewer seats than the community center, pulsates with rock music and strobe lights, so my chances of falling asleep during this performance are probably slim. But given the WELCOME, NEW TROUBLEMAKER TRAINEES! banner hanging above the front row, and the front row's close proximity to the stage, becoming *part* of the performance isn't out of the question. And that would be way worse.

Lemon doesn't seem to share my concern. He heads right for our section, chomping on popcorn and slurping soda. I'm checking the last row for empty seats when there's a tap on my shoulder.

I turn around. Mr. Tempest, the quiet teacher who sat at Annika's table at dinner the other night, stands behind me. He wears a black wool coat buttoned to his chin and holds two ice-cream cones—strawberry in his left hand and vanilla in his right. His mouth moves, but the music's so loud I can't hear what he says.

"Sorry?" I shout.

His lips press together. His nostrils widen. "*Have* you *stepped* in *gum*?"

"What?!" I yell.

"Did the *soles* of your *shoes* come into contact with a previously *chewed*, *unnatural*, *sticky substance* that has since *solidified*, permanently locking your *feet* in their current *positions*?"

I look down. Lift one heel, then the other.

"Oh, never mind." Mr. Tempest pushes past me. "Some boy wonder."

For some reason, his disappointment's reassuring. I hurry toward the stage and join Lemon in the front row. Abe and Gabby are already there. Elinor arrives a few seconds later and takes the last empty seat, on the aisle. She comes alone and looks straight ahead without talking to anyone.

I lean toward Lemon. "What's her story?"

He follows my nod to Elinor. Shakes his head. "Don't."

"Don't what?"

"Think about it. Unless you're into being the lowly servant of Kilter's reigning ice queen."

Ice queen? As in cold? Unapproachable? Our interaction's been brief, but still. Elinor didn't strike me as either of those things.

Before I can press him further, the lights go out. The music stops. The audience falls silent. And then slowly, the stage is illuminated. It glows a shimmery blue, reminding me of a skating rink. The back of the stage descends and then rises up—with four Troublemakers playing electric guitar, drums, and piano. Unlike the loud rock that shook the pavilion moments ago, the music now is quieter, serious. The beats are steady, the notes low. It's like the music you hear in a movie, when the bad guy follows the good guy close behind without the good guy knowing. You know something major's about to go down, but you don't know exactly what.

A long, thin section of center stage descends. It reappears holding ten Troublemakers. They wear jeans, silver sneakers, shimmery gray sweatshirts, and sunglasses—even though we're indoors. They stand with their feet spread and hands behind their backs, and look straight ahead.

The music continues, low and steady, while the stage rises. Once the stage is in place, it stops. For a few seconds, the audience members are silent, the Troublemakers before us as still as statues.

And then: chaos.

The band explodes. Strobe lights pulsate. Spotlights follow the Troublemakers, who scatter across the stage. One races to the far end, climbs a twenty-foot ladder, and takes a gleaming bow and arrow from a sheath on his back. On the opposite end, a second Troublemaker steps onto a swinging platform that looks like a clock pendulum—only it lifts and spins. As the music grows louder, faster, the swinging Troublemaker holds up a silver disc. The spotlights shift to the other Troublemaker, who raises his loaded bow and arrow.

"No way!" Lemon shouts over the squealing bass and pounding drums.

I agree. The archer aims for the silver disc. It's a moving, impossible shot.

The archer pulls back, releases the arrow. Spotlights follow the long silver dart as it slices through the air . . . and hits the spinning disc's center.

An enormous, rotating globe lowers from the domed ceiling. It looks like a disco ball at first, but then the tiny mirrored squares, which must be digital, are replaced with words:

BULL'S-EYE!

And the crowd goes wild.

More demonstrations follow. There's a fire starter who blankets the stage in flames. An acrobat who tumbles and soars past a series of blockades set up in a makeshift house. A painter who sketches the audience onto concrete walls that rise up around the stage's edge. There are also a few I don't understand, like one Troublemaker who belches into a microphone as the overhead globe turns into a clock and counts to sixty seconds, and another who removes her sunglasses and simply stares at the crowd without blinking.

The whole thing is a cross between a rock concert and a circus. I don't get it . . . but that doesn't mean I'm not entertained.

Eventually, the music lowers to non-earsplitting decibels. The performers return to their original positions. Every spotlight but one goes out.

And Annika takes the stage. She wears dark jeans, a glittery gray sweater-coat that falls to her ankles, and silver high-heeled boots. She smiles and waves as the audience claps and cheers.

"Welcome!" she declares. "Enjoy the show?"

Cheers turn to screams. I cover my ears.

"I'd like to say that your peers prepared long and hard for this performance, but the truth is, they have this much fun every single day." Still smiling, Annika looks at our section. "And soon, Kilter Academy's newest students will too."

There's more applause. I release my ears and lean over to Lemon.

"What's she talking about?" I yell.

"No idea!"

"So without further ado," Annika continues, "let the eighteenth annual Troublemaker Tutor Assignments commence!"

The pavilion lights dim. Soon all I can see is the rotating ball suspended from the ceiling. It drops several feet, then stops.

"You're about to join one of Kilter's six illustrious groups." Annika's voice cuts through the darkness. "In no particular order, they are the Dramatists . . . the Biohazards . . . Les Artistes . . ."

Glowing logos appear on the ball, which seems to be some sort of screen. There are drama masks. An outline of the human torso. An easel and canvas bearing a human skull.

". . . the Fire Starters . . . the Athletes . . ."

A flickering flame. A winged sneaker.

". . . and last but not least, the Sniper Squad!"

And a hand grenade.

"Your tutors are older Troublemakers from your group. They've been chosen for you based on your individual talents, and they will help you grow those talents through one-on-one lessons and personalized feedback." Annika pauses. "Are we ready?"

The crowd cheers as another light shoots up from below, illuminating a circle of clear, high-backed chairs in the center of the stage, just beneath the ball. As we watch, one familiar face, then another and another, appears on the round screen.

"Austin Baker!" Annika declares. "Carla Simmons! Sam Fitzgerald! Priscilla Todd! Lucas Horn! Please join us onstage!"

A camera focuses on several Troublemakers I recognize from classes. It catches their chins dropping, smiles forming, and excitement growing as they launch out of their seats, and projects every reaction on-screen for the entire pavilion to see. They land in the clear chairs, and the camera takes turns zeroing in on each of their faces. Their images rotate above them, framed by their names, ages, and hometowns in big white letters.

The Troublemaker performers gather around my classmates. Austin, Carla, Sam, Priscilla, and Lucas, still seated in a circle, begin to spin slowly. The performers look straight ahead, their expressions blank. The audience grows quiet. I don't know these kids personally, but I'm nervous for them anyway, and wipe my damp forehead with my sleeve.

Austin's chair stops in front of the belcher. The camera focuses on the back of the chair as the glowing image of a human torso appears.

"Gas Attendant!" Annika exclaims to whoops and whistles. "Brilliant!"

The belching Troublemaker grins. Pats Austin on the back. Leads him to a table and presents him with a silver ski parka. On the jacket's sleeve is a patch with the Kilter Academy logo and the same torso image displayed on the round screen.

Annika matches each of the other kids with an older Troublemaker. The first-year Troublemakers have the same talents as their individual tutors, but no two first-years have the exact same skill. Together, they all form the Biohazard group.

Next, Annika calls out five new names, one of which I recognize right away.

"Abraham Hansen!"

Abe jumps out of his seat and runs onstage. During his turn, the spinning, clear throne stops in front of the Troublemaker painter. The easel-and-skull logo appears on the ball.

"Aerosol Assaulter!" Annika sings. "Welcome to Les Artistes!"

On and on it goes. Gabby stops in front of the strange staring girl. Elinor stops in front of the guy whose performance was convincing us he was a blind psychic before confessing he was neither. Our class is fairly evenly divided, with about five first-years joining each group. Every pairing is met with cheers and screams, the loudest of which comes from the pavilion section with the most members of the particular group just announced.

Now, Annika's introduction was pretty clear, so on some level, I get what's happening. But all the noise and flashing lights and other hoopla must be more distracting than I realized, because for some reason, I don't process what this really means until it's Lemon's turn . . . and the chair stops in front of the kid who started fires around other Troublemakers.

"Flame Thrower!"

Lemon's paired with the fire starter.

And I'm about to be exposed to the entire school.

"Seamus Hinkle!" Annika shouts.

My stomach drops. My eyes lock on those opened wide on the round overhead screen, register the words over and under the bright red face.

SEAMUS HINKLE

12 YEARS OLD

CLOUDVIEW, NEW YORK

I hold my breath, listen for other names . . . but there aren't any.

"Uh-oh!" Annika exclaims. "I think someone's shy! Let's give our newest new student a warm Kilter welcome!"

I want to run. Hide. Or, better yet, die—just like I should've my first night here. Taking my secret to the grave would be a million times better than broadcasting it in front of hundreds of kids.

The crowd claps and calls my name. My feet, ignoring screaming protests from my brain, lead me onstage and to a clear, high-backed chair. The others remain empty. I look down as I start spinning, dreading the shocked gasps and looks that will soon fill the pavilion. I wonder which Troublemaker the chair will stop before, since unless that spotlight bulb was out and we missed it, no one died during the performance.

The spinning slows. My eyes squeeze shut. Annika starts to say the terrible, awful word I still can't believe describes me.

"M . . . arksman!"

My heart stops.

Marksman.

Not murderer.

"Welcome to the Sniper Squad!" Annika adds.

The pavilion erupts. My eyelids snap up. The archer who hit the swinging bull's-eye from a hundred feet away stands before me.

"Seamus Hinkle," he says with a grin. "I think we're going to make some major trouble together."

Chapter 9

DEMERITS: 100
GOLD STARS: 45

My tutor's name is Ike, and he doesn't waste any time getting started. He leads me offstage as soon as the spot-light shifts from us to Annika, and we hurry outside.

"Are you sure the ceremony's over?" I ask, jogging to keep up. "Shouldn't we hang around to make sure we don't miss anything?"

"And forfeit a head start? I don't think so."

Ike veers left, toward a small parking lot—and a golf cart. He hops in and pats the front seat for me to join him. I stop a few feet before the cart and glance over my shoulder. A fireworks display lights up the gray, early-morning sky over the Performance Pavilion.

"What are you afraid of?" he asks.

That Annika only said "marksman" instead of "murderer" to keep from terrifying the audience. That Ike wears a black parka with a blank sleeve patch, while all the other tutors wear silver parkas with distinct emblems. That he's used his bows and arrows to kill before, and that he's about to do so again. That if I leave with him, there won't be any witnesses to confirm what happened and make sure Mom and Dad get the right story.

"Ever ridden in a golf cart before?"

I turn back. "Once. With my dad at the Cloudview Putt 'n' Play."

"Did you go from zero to sixty in eight point two seconds?"

"We didn't go from zero to six in ten minutes."

Ike smiles. Tilts his head toward the empty seat.

As fireworks boom behind us, I remind myself that my K-Pak's in my backpack. If necessary, I can shoot Lemon or Annika a quick note letting them know what's about to happen. And then I climb into the cart.

Speed isn't the only difference between this cart and the one I rode in with Dad. This cart has a curved, clear roof. The seats are soft white leather. The dashboard is made of wood so polished I can see my lips tremble the way they do when I'm scared but trying to hide it. A clear seat belt automatically slides around my waist and across my chest. Once I'm buckled, a digital 3-D map forms over the dash. I recognize the Kanteen and classroom building before Ike touches one edge of the map. It shifts and zooms in on an empty field rimmed in trees. Ike touches the field, spins it around, and flicks the map once more.

"Ready?" he asks.

I nod.

"Go!"

I'm pretty sure tires leave pavement, though I'm holding on too tightly to lean down and look. The cart zooms from the parking lot, zigzags around trees and buildings. I try to smile at Ike, to show him traveling at warp speed is cool with me, but the force pushes my head and torso back into the leather seat.

Then, as quickly as it took off, the golf cart stops. We're at the edge of the field we just saw on the map. But unlike its digital image, the field's not empty. Lined up from one end to the other are twenty or so figures wearing skirts and blouses, khakis and sweaters. At first I think they're real people, but as we step out of the cart and walk toward them, I realize they're mannequins. Only where their plastic heads should be, red apples sit instead.

I stop short. Ike turns around.

"I thought we'd start closer," he says with a shrug. "But you can shoot from there if you want."

I shake my head, step back. "I can't shoot."

"Think of it more as practicing aim and focus. That's ninety-nine percent of what archery is, after all." He follows my wide-eyed stare to the apple-topped mannequins. "I know you're used to produce being the weapon and not the target, but Annika said you'd mastered that skill and were ready for something more serious. Which, by the way, is also more fun."

I look at him. "Annika told you to bring me here?"

"No."

I release a small sigh of relief. Of course she didn't. She's too nice to recommend something like this.

"She told me to let you loose in the Kilter garden. But I

thought it was better to start in an open space and minimize casualties."

My heart drops. He turns on one heel and keeps walking. I look around for an escape, but we're in the middle of nowhere. Even if I got away, where would I go? Deciding it's best to keep an armed man happy, I start after Ike.

"So, what exactly does a Troublemaker tutor do?" I ask when I reach him, hoping to keep things light. He's assembling his arsenal five feet from an innocent mannequin in a long purple dress.

"What any tutor does. Helps you get better at something."

"And you're going to help me get better at archery?"

"Among other things, yes."

"But I've never shot an arrow before. How do you know I need help?"

I'm genuinely curious about why I'm being tutored in something I've never even tried, but Ike stops polishing his bow and looks at me like I'm being a smart aleck. Which, believe me, I'm not.

"Good question," he says. "I guess there's only one way to find out."

He reaches into the duffel bag on the ground and pulls out a red plastic bow and an arrow with a suction-cup tip. They remind me of toys a five-year-old would play with in a game of cowboys and Indians. I must look confused, because Ike explains.

"Every student has to start somewhere. As you get better, so will your weapons."

I don't want to get better. I don't even want to start. But my tutor's silver arrows still hang from his belt loop, and they look even sharper up close. So I take the plastic set and try to look happy about it.

"Right elbow back," Ike instructs. "Left arm straight. Fingers tight. Hold it steady."

I do as I'm told. The hardest part's holding steady, as my entire body's shaking.

"Just aim for the mannequin," Ike says. "Don't worry about the apples."

Easier said than done. But I close my eyes and release the arrow. There's a soft thump as contact's made.

"Not bad," Ike says.

I open my eyes. The arrow's suction-cup tip has stuck to the toe of the mannequin's shiny black shoe.

"Not great, either . . . but we can work with it."

For the next hour, I listen to Ike and make my way down the long line of targets. I hit each one but only where life-threatening damage wouldn't be done if the suction cup were replaced with a metal tip—like fingers and toes, shoulders and shins. If Ike's disappointed by my amateur aim, he doesn't let on. He's surprisingly patient and encouraging. The experience might even be fun if this were simply gym class at Cloudview.

When we take a break, Ike excuses himself to answer some K-Mail, and I find a rock several yards away from the firing range. I sit, take my K-Pak from my backpack, and load my own messages. I'm about to open one from Houdini about next week's math assignment when a bang sounds somewhere behind me. It's so loud birds scatter from the treetops.

Without thinking, I drop the K-Pak and snatch the plastic bow and arrow from the holster slung across my back. I load the arrow as I spin toward the noise.

And then I fire.

"Awesome!" Ike yells.

I lower the bow and squint. He's standing near the golf cart and wearing what looks like a black shield over his torso. He turns to the side so I can see the arrow stuck to the middle of his chest.

"The second I set off that firecracker, you totally went into auto archer mode! I knew you had it in you!"

The arrow's still stuck to his chest as he starts jogging. He waves for me to meet him halfway, so I force my feet to move. When we reach Mannequin Row, he opens his mouth to say something else just as I open mine to apologize.

But we're both interrupted by another sound. This one's a rumble that starts soft and quickly grows louder. Before I can ask what it is, a motorized two-person bicycle shoots out from the woods and skids to a stop next to the golf cart. Two men in khaki pants, red-checkered shirts, and red fanny packs dismount and stride toward us.

Ike turns toward me so his back's to them. He plucks the arrow from his chest and shoves it into my hand, then unzips and rezips his jacket so the plastic shield is hidden inside.

"Be cool," he whispers. "Just practice."

Like not worrying about the apples, this is a tall order. But I do my best to point and shoot at the mannequins while he waves to the approaching men.

"Good morning!" he calls out.

"It *is* a good morning, isn't it?" one of the men says pleasantly when they reach us.

"Especially for getting into trouble," the second man says.

"Is it?" Ike asks. "I just meant weather-wise. No one's getting into trouble here."

"No?" the first man says.

"Nope. Seamus and I were just having our first tutoring session." When Ike speaks again, his voice is quieter. "Between you and me, the kid needs all the help he can get."

Guessing this is some sort of cue, I load an arrow and shift my aim. The arrow releases and lands with a plop by my feet.

"So it seems," the second man says.

"By the way," Ike says, "sweet ride. Is it new?"

This distracts the men instantly, and Ike walks with them back to their bicycle. As they talk, I continue shooting, careful to avoid any direct contact with the mannequins. By the time Ike returns, the ground's covered in red plastic arrows.

"They're like German shepherd puppies," he says with a sigh.

I glance over my shoulder. The men and bicycle are gone. "Who were they?"

"The Good Samaritans. Kilter's version of security."

"What do they do?"

"Stop Troublemakers and report bad behavior as necessary." Ike leans down and scoops up a handful of arrows. "They're pretty good when they're paying attention. But like baby guard dogs, it doesn't take much to make them lose focus."

I don't get it. "But aren't we *supposed* to make trouble? Isn't that why we're here?"

"It is."

"Then why do they want to stop us?"

"To keep us sharp." Ike stands, then hands me a cluster of arrows. "If you can avoid Good Samaritans at Kilter, you can avoid parents and other adults in the real world. It's another form of training—and a costly one at that. If you're caught, you lose troublemaking privileges—and the opportunity to earn demerits and credits—for a specified amount of time. Some Trouble-makers never bounce back."

"Why'd they come here?" I ask. The targets are strange, but I'm still shooting toy weapons. This seems more like playtime than it does serious troublemaking.

"To check you out," Ike says with a grin. "Because unlike

what I told them, you, my friend, are off to a great start."

He says this like it's good news. Like it's something I should be happy about—even proud of.

But as I reload a plastic arrow, all I can think is that if its tip was metal instead of rubber, I'd have just become a murderer for the second time.

Chapter 10

DEMERITS: 110
GOLD STARS: 45

We train until the sun begins to set. Ike's so happy with my progress he awards me ten demerits and tells me to treat myself to something nice at the Kommissary. Instead I treat myself to some alone time in my room. Lemon's still out with his tutor when I get back, and I take advantage of the time alone to use the phone.

"Hoodlum Hotline, how may I direct your call?"

"I'd like to be connected to the main operator," I say. "Please."

"You're talking to her."

"No, not the main operator of Hoodlum Hotline, the main operator of—" I stop when the bedroom door opens. Lemon comes into the room, drops his backpack to the floor, and falls on the bed face-first. I'm not sure he even knows I'm there, but I cover the mouthpiece with my hand anyway and whisper, "I'll take this outside."

"Son, is there a problem?"

A group of older Troublemakers are having a rowdy spitball-shooting contest in the hallway. Not wanting to be overheard—or shot—I hurry to the exit and enter the main courtyard.

"I'd like to call my parents, please. Eliot and Judith Hinkle." I carefully recite the number.

"That's a lovely thought. I'm sure they'd be touched."

This is followed by a long pause. I wait for ringing and prepare what I'll say once Mom or Dad picks up.

"Is there anything else?"

"Mom?"

"Are you a hairless, three-legged Chihuahua named Rodolfo?"

"What? No."

"Then I'm not your mother."

The operator. She's still on the line. "Sorry," I say. "I didn't realize you hadn't dialed yet."

"No problem. And I won't. Dial, that is."

"But this is the only phone in our room. It has only one button. How do I call them?"

"You don't."

"But Houdini said we could."

"And you believed him?" she says with a snort. "You'll see your folks in a few weeks, on Parents' Day. Now, if you'll excuse me, the switchboard's lighting up like a carnival. Thanks for calling Hoodlum Hotline!"

The line goes dead.

I'm about to turn around and head back inside when a noise stops me. It's a soft whine that sounds a little like wind whistling through trees . . . except the air's still. As I listen, the whine grows to a moan, then a wail. It seems to come from the other side of the courtyard. My brain says it's none of my business, but my feet lead away from the dorm anyway. When the noise gets louder, they move faster.

It doesn't take long to locate the noise's source: Carter Montgomery. Next to me, he's the shortest Troublemaker in

Annika had seen me hit my targets in the field earlier today.

"Homesick?"

I spin toward the voice. Elinor, the pretty redhead, sits cross-legged on a bench behind me. In the light of a tall lamppost, I can see an open book balanced on her knees.

"It's okay if you are," she says.

I glance back at the fountain, where another Troublemaker is trying to cry fake tears as Annika and the others watch. I hurry toward Elinor before they hear her—or notice me.

"I'm not," I say when I reach her. "Why do you think I am?"

Her eyes lower to my hand. I look down, surprised to see I'm still holding the black phone. In the commotion, I'd forgotten all about it.

She closes her book and stands. "Want to walk?"

I watch her start down the sidewalk. Does she expect me to follow her? Do I *want* to follow her?

Two older Troublemakers play laser tag in the grass behind the bench. In between blasts, they joke and chuckle.

"Mommy, I *miss* you," one calls out.

"Daddy, *please* come get me! I need my binky and ba-ba and—"

our class. And he's standing in the small spotlights of a stone fountain, crying.

I hold my breath and watch from behind a tree several feet away. He's not bleeding. He doesn't appear to be under attack by other Troublemakers. So do I ask if he's okay? Offer to help? Call the Hoodlum Hotline and report a Troublemaker in distress?

As I debate, Carter's knees fold. He sinks to the grass, lowers his head forward, and pounds the ground with both fists. The wailing gives way to hiccups and shoulder shudders.

"Bravo!"

I jump. Carter sits up. Annika emerges from the shadows, clapping. Mr. Tempest follows close behind, head down and shoulders slumped.

"Impressive performance," she says.

Carter stands and wipes the tears from his face.

"You might want to tone down the volume and delay the collapse, but still. Very convincing." She turns to Carter's tutor, who stands nearby with three other members of the Dramatists group. "Nice work, Mark."

Mark takes a slight bow. Carter beams. I think this is a very strange display . . . but for some reason, it also makes me wish

I shoot down the sidewalk. My hecklers, who had obviously overheard my phone call, fall silent.

"I'm Elinor," she says when I catch up.

"I know." Then, feeling my cheeks warm under her curious glance, I add, "From the tutor assignment ceremony today. And class the other day."

"Oh." She looks away. One hand travels behind her back, brushes the green satin ribbon tied at the end of her braid.

"Houdini got my robot cuff links," I say sympathetically. "I still don't know how he did it—they were pinned to my sleeves. How did he unscrew them? And pull them out? While I was wearing them?"

She smiles, which makes me smile too.

"What's funny?" I ask.

"Nothing."

"You looked like you were about to laugh."

She stops walking and faces me. "You're talking fast."

"So?"

"So you seem nervous." She pauses. "Are you?"

Nervous? Me? I'm enrolled in a top secret professional trouble-making camp. I killed my substitute teacher. My roommate's an arsonist. I'm following a girl who did who-knows-what to who-knows-who, whom I know nothing about, and it's getting darker with each passing second. Why would I be nervous?

Elinor keeps walking. "Are you close to them?"

I hurry to keep up. "Who?"

"Your parents."

"Oh. Yes. Very."

Then I think about it. *Am* I close to them? I mean, they're always around . . . but they're my parents. That's where they're supposed to be. And though Dad and I sometimes kick back and watch movies, or talk about the Yankees and Giants, Mom and I don't really spend a lot of quality time together. Unless you count the time she spends overseeing my chores-and-homework progress, and expressing her disapproval, which I guess I do. And as for talking, our conversations are usually fairly one-sided, with her firing off question after question about school while giving me two seconds to respond to each one. But that's normal, isn't it? After all, parents and kids aren't supposed to be best friends.

"Are you?" I ask Elinor. "Close to yours?"

Instead of answering, she grabs my arm and yanks me through a thick curtain of drooping branches.

"Hey!" I try to pull away. "What are you—"

She clamps one hand over my mouth. I might bite her fingers to make her let go, except I'm instantly distracted by the fact that they smell like raspberries.

"Don't move," she whispers.

She holds her eyes to mine. Then, apparently deciding I'm not about to run screaming from the trees, she lowers her hand and leans toward the branches. I peer over her shoulder and through a narrow opening. Four Good Samaritans circle a nearby pond; two jump in, fanny packs and all, and the others remove tanks and hoses from behind a bush.

"Let's go," Elinor says. "While they're busy."

She gets up and starts for the other side of the leafy canopy. I watch the drenched Good Samaritans emerge from the water with a dripping Troublemaker. The Troublemaker wears a wet suit, mask, and snorkel. The hoses wrapped around his body lead to the tank onshore, which makes me believe the Good Samaritans have just stopped him from draining the pond.

"I thought you wanted to talk to your parents," Elinor says. She stands next to me again.

"I did," I say. "I do."

"There's a secret phone. A real one, with twelve buttons. I know where it is."

I jump up. "How?"

She doesn't answer. Instead she smiles, then slips through the curtain of leaves.

Heart thumping, I race after her. I fly across grass and burst through branches. Weave through trees and hurdle rocks. As we run, Elinor pulls farther and farther ahead. Eventually, she blends in with the descending darkness.

I catch up with her only once, at a river she doesn't immediately know how to cross. Seeing me behind her, she bends her knees and leaps, landing lightly on a rock no bigger than my hand. She continues across the remaining rapids that way, hopping from one small rock to the next as easily as if they were hopscotch squares and the water was pavement. She doesn't look back again, which is good, since my leap lands me face-first in river silt.

"I'll be right there!" I yell, wiping mud from my eyes.

"Go left on the other side!" she shouts. Each word is softer, more distant than the one before. "When you reach the field of sunflowers, turn right and look for the bunker!"

It takes a while—and eight additional spills—but eventually I cross the river and follow the rest of my instructions.

Unfortunately, I don't find sunflowers, a bunker, or a phone.

Worst of all, I don't find Elinor.

Chapter 11

DEMERITS: 130
GOLD STARS: 60

Stop!"

I shoot up in bed.

"Drop!"

Grab the cup and canister from my nightstand.

"R—"

And fire.

Lemon stumbles back. Blinks the sleep from his eyes. Shakes the water from his hair.

"Again?" he says with a sigh.

"Again." I stand up for a better shot at the burning trash can. The remaining flames fizzle out under the white foam. "But look. All we lost this time is some used tissues and candy wrappers. No big deal."

He flops on his bed. Puts his elbows on his knees, his forehead in his hands. "Dude. I'm so going to kill you."

For a second I think he's mad that I intervened, but then I realize he's seriously concerned.

"The Kilter Pocket Extinguisher has a ten-foot range," I say. "I can reach every corner of the room without getting out of bed. As long as you keep yelling in your sleep so I wake up, we're good."

His head slowly lifts. Water droplets slide down his forehead, off his nose. "The what?"

"Kilter Pocket Extinguisher." I hand him the small silver canister. "For your on-the-go blaze-blanketing needs."

"Where'd you get this?"

"The Kommissary. They'd just gotten a new shipment when I stopped there last night."

"And you bought it for me?"

"I bought it for us," I say. "So we can both sleep a little easier."

He turns the canister over and rubs his thumb across the shiny surface. "You should be saving your credits for fancy bows and arrows."

"What good are fancy bows and arrows if I'm not alive to use them?"

I mean this as a joke. Thankfully, Lemon seems to take it that way. The corner of his mouth lifts as he stands and hands me the fire extinguisher.

"Let me make it up to you."

"You really don't have to."

"Yes, I do." He opens his closet and slides out a white Styrofoam cooler. "I make a mean breakfast burrito. What do you say?"

I start to say no thanks, but stop. Because I'm not sure . . . but I think Lemon and I might be bonding.

"That sounds great. Thanks."

Lemon starts a new, controlled fire. While he cooks, I check my e-mail and find a new message.

TO: shinkle@kilteracademy.org
FROM: kommissary@kilteracademy.org
SUBJECT: Credits to Burn?

> Hiya, Seamus!
>
> Thanks for swinging by the Kommissary and picking up a Kilter Pocket Extinguisher. We hope it helps you make tons of trouble! And if you want a little assistance with starting fires to put out, we totally recommend the Kilter Super Sparker. It can turn up the temperature anywhere, anytime!

I click on the flashing camera and a video begins. A smiling kid holds what look like two tiny tin cups up to the camera. He puts one on the tip of his thumb and the other on the tip of his middle finger, and snaps. A silver spark pops from his hand. Wondering if Lemon knows about this, I stop the video and keep reading.

> Between your weekly allowance and completed homework assignments, you've earned a few more demerits. Unfortunately, you've also contacted the Hoodlum Hotline and earned a few more gold stars. But no worries! You're still in the game. Our records show that you currently have 130 demerits and 60

gold stars, which gives you 70 credits. You dropped 20 credits on the Kilter Pocket Extinguisher, so you have 50 credits left. That's more than enough to buy the Kilter Super Sparker, which is a sizzling steal at 30 credits!

See you soon? We hope so!

At Your Service,

The Kommissary Krew

I close the e-mail. Lemon's still cooking, so I make a mental note to tell him about the Super Sparker, and then I take a shower and get dressed. By the time I come out of the bathroom, the sun's up and breakfast's ready.

And he wasn't kidding: The burrito's *mean.* It's stuffed with eggs and cheese and three types of beans. It's so good, when I clean my plate and he offers to make me another one, I accept.

"Do you cook a lot at home?" I ask as he cracks two eggs at once.

He nods. "We have an old gas stove. You need matches to light it. Cooking is the one way I can play with fire inside the house without my parents freaking out."

This reminds me of my conversation with Elinor last night. "Are you close?" I ask. "You and your parents?"

"Depends what you mean by close." He lifts the frying pan, flips the eggs.

"After you're done cooking, do you sit down and eat together? And, like, talk?"

"Yes. All the time. Then when we're done eating, we talk some more. And some more after that." He dumps a can of beans into the pan. "My parents are big on communicating. They never stop."

I wonder if that's why Lemon doesn't say much here. Maybe he likes not being forced to make constant conversation. Just in case, I don't ask any more questions now. I simply watch him cook, and thank him when he hands me another burrito.

I've just finished the second helping when he checks his K-Pak.

"Uh-oh," he says. "Bio's meeting early in the library today."

"Why's that bad?" I ask, licking my fingers.

"The library's across campus. And we were supposed to be there ten minutes ago." He tosses his K-Pak on the bed. "We better haul."

So we do. Or more accurately, Lemon hauls, and I, weighed down by the five pounds of burrito now in my stomach, huff and puff and lag behind. By the time I reach the library entrance, he's already seated inside.

I stop to catch my breath and peer through the double glass doors. My classmates are scattered throughout the large room; some sit at tables, others on couches and chairs. Their heads are bent as they read and write. Several older students are also working, but no one stands out as a librarian or potential teacher. I'm thinking they're very well behaved for bad kids without chaperones when I see the digital sign flashing just inside the entrance.

YOU'RE ENTERING KILTER'S ONLY NOISE-FREE ZONE.

PLEASE RESPECT YOUR FELLOW TROUBLEMAKERS!

Once I can breathe normally, I go inside. Lemon's already slouched in an armchair on the other side of the room with his eyes closed, so I tiptoe to my nearest classmate: Abraham Hansen, Aerosol Assaulter.

I tap his shoulder. "Excuse me? Do you think you could—"

"Shh!"

I glance up. A girl at the next table looks at me and shakes her head.

Sorry, I mouth.

She returns to her book. I return to Abe. He holds up a notepad. It's filled with boxed-in drawings, like a comic strip. In the first box, three stick figures sit at a table, reading. In the second, a shorter stick figure enters the room. His mouth is a thin line that tilts up on one side, like he's smirking. In the third box, the shorter stick figure, now on top of the table, pounds his stick arms to his stick chest and raises his chin. Above his open mouth, "BURRRRPPPPPP!!!!!" is written around a dark, swirling cloud. In the next box, the stick figures flee the table, horrified.

Abe lowers the notepad. Writes "5 Demerits" above the toxic cloud. Holds it up again.

"I don't get it," I say. "So we're supposed to—"

"Shh!"

Abe turns the page to another series of drawings. This one looks a lot like the first, except instead of the cloud bursting from the stick figure's mouth, it shoots out from where his rear end would be if he had one. Next to that cloud Abe writes "10 Demerits."

Then, as if the universe could sense my confusion, the room's silence is shattered by a bang—no, a *roar.* I jump. Abe covers his ears. The girl at the next table winces like she's been punched in the gut. The noise doesn't last more than five seconds, but it feels like days.

When it's over, there are giggles. Whispers. I look around for the culprit, and so does everyone else.

Except for Samara, our biology teacher. She stands by a tall bookshelf labeled FAMOUS RABBLE-ROUSERS THROUGHOUT HISTORY. When our eyes meet, she nods to a door behind her, then disappears through it.

I don't know what she wants, but I follow her into the custodial closet anyway. Bodily noises make me uncomfortable, and any excuse to get away from them is a good one.

"You're late," she says when I close the door behind me.

"I know. My roommate had issues and then we had breakfast and—"

"Enough." She holds up one hand. "Normally, I don't tolerate tardiness—I don't care who you are. But because you're Annika's golden child, I'm going to do you a huge favor and fill you in on what you've missed."

"Thanks," I say, trying not to dwell on the "golden child" reference.

She hikes up the left leg of her jeans. Taped to the skin below her knee is a round silver pouch. She lifts her right foot and taps the pouch with her heel.

The custodial closet fills with a shorter, softer version of what we just heard in the library.

"A whoopee cushion?" I say. "That's what made that noise?"

She drops her cuff. The cushion disappears.

"It doesn't matter how old you are—or how mature. Bodily noises, real or phony, will get you every time. Used correctly, they're some of the most powerful weapons in combating controlling adults. One unexpected wrong noise can strip your parents of all logic, reason, and memory ten times more effectively than any crying fit or temper tantrum." She looks up at me. "Your task in this class is to earn twenty demerits. Burps are five demerits, far—"

"The others are ten," I finish quickly. That word makes me even more uncomfortable than the actual act does. "I know. But I don't have a whoopee cushion."

"It's a K-Pouch. And neither does anyone else out there."

My eyes widen. "You mean we're supposed to—*I'm* supposed to . . . ? In front of all those people, you want me to—"

"You don't have to really *do* those things. Just make the noises. Preferably without anyone knowing it's you."

She reaches past me and opens the door. I shuffle backward. When the door closes again, I force myself to turn around and face the silent library.

The assignment's embarrassing, but I'd still like to make a good impression on Samara. She *is* my teacher, after all, and we haven't gotten off to the best start. So I find an empty lounge chair in one corner of the room. I turn it around until it faces the wall, climb over one arm, and slide down the seat.

And for the next forty-five minutes, I try. I really do. I take deep breaths. Stick out my tongue. Think about Dr Pepper and Mountain Dew. But every time I'm about to blow, someone else does, shattering the silence—and my concentration. It takes several minutes to work up to each attempt; before long, class is over, and time's up.

Feeling both relieved and disappointed, I climb out of the chair and start across the library. Up ahead, Lemon walks and whispers with Gabby and Abe. I start jogging to catch up.

And then I stop. My belly, still full of burrito, turns. I hold my breath and stand perfectly still, but it only turns faster. Then it twists. Cramps. Growls. My face burns as I clamp both hands over the noise's source. Frantic, I scan the library for a bathroom, but there are only two doors: one for the cleaning closet and another marked ARCHIVES. I noticed a bathroom when I came into the building, but it's three hallways from here. And I don't have that kind of time.

A dozen older students remain in the library. They don't look up as I pass, but I try to smile anyway. The below-belt growling grows louder, and if they hear it, I want to reassure them everything's fine.

Even though it is *so* not. My stomach's on the brink of explosion, and it takes every bit of strength I have to walk—not sprint—to the Archives room. Reaching the door, I fling it open and dart inside. The small room's filled with metal shelves lined with books and binders. Desperate to get as far away from the rest of the library as possible, I dash down the nearest aisle and into a corner.

Beans, beans, they're good for your heart! The more you eat, the more you—

My body finishes the chorus right on cue. The noise is loud, the force strong. I think the concrete wall I lean against shakes, though I'm also trembling from fear and exertion, so it's hard to be sure.

But then it's over. And I feel like a new man.

I wait a few seconds to make sure there's not a second wave. When my stomach remains calm, I sigh in relief and head for the door.

Which is now blocked. By Samara, who stands with her hands over her nose and mouth and her legs spread and glued to the wood behind her. A messenger bag lies open on one side of her feet, and a cup of coffee is splattered on the other. Her eyes are wide, her breathing heavy.

"Congratulations, Seamus Hinkle," she half gasps, half whispers. "Maybe Annika's right about you after all."

Chapter 12

DEMERITS: 250
GOLD STARS: 60

TO: parsippany@cloudviewschools.net
FROM: shinkle@kilteracademy.org
SUBJECT: Another One Bites the Dust

Dear Miss Parsippany,

Well, I did it again. The other day, after biology class, I did something bad to another teacher. It was so bad, she froze and blushed and practically cried. I can't really tell you HOW I did this (trust me, you don't want to know), but I CAN say that it's a week later, and I still feel terrible.

Like the apple hitting you and the balls hitting Fern, what happened with Samara was an accident. I've tried to make up for it anyway, by being the best student I can be . . . but classes here are weird. What we learn is weird too.

Take music. At Cloudview, this class is for listening to Beethoven and counting beats and playing "Greensleeves" on Mr. O'Mally's keyboard. But here? Music is for whistling without moving your lips. That's what we did the other day. For two hours.

The other classes are just as strange. In gym we did wind sprints through campus while older students disguised as adults chased us. In language arts we brushed up on pig Latin and learned pig French, which is similar to pig Latin but adds an extra "ay" to the end of every word. In art we drew pictures so scary they'd give parents nightmares for weeks—which was the point.

I still don't get what I'm supposed to do with

these skills out in the real world, but I'm playing along. Because it makes my teachers happy. And because eventually, the semester will end. I'll go home. My parents will think I'm reformed, and I'll do everything I can to convince them that's true. And Kilter will just be this weird place near the North Pole where I once spent a few weeks.

At least, that's what I'm hoping.

Sincerely,

Seamus Hinkle

"Love letter?"

I jump. The K-Pak slips from my grip. Ike swoops in and catches it before it hits the ground.

"Ladies dig a guy with a romantic side." He grins and holds out the K-Pak. "Who is she?"

I open my mouth to explain, but then stop. Do I really want to tell my troublemaking tutor that I write e-mails I can never send to my dead substitute teacher? Won't that remind him that I'm a murderer, which is the one thing I wish everyone would forget?

"Elinor," I say. Hers is the first name I think of.

"The ice queen?" Ike shivers. "Better bundle up."

"What's that?" I nod to the long silver sheath hanging at his side. Whatever it is, I'd rather talk about it than any feelings I may or may not have for my prettiest classmate.

Ike removes the sheath and holds it toward me. "A gift."

I smile. "What for?"

"For just being you."

This doesn't seem like a very good reason, but I don't want to be rude. So I take the sheath and undo the Velcro running down its center. When I see the skinny shaft, the comma-shaped trigger, my reflected face turning white in the gleaming steel, I squeeze both ends of the gift to keep from shoving it back at Ike.

"A gun?" I say.

"Not quite." Ike drops to his knees next to me. "A Kilter Painter 1000. The best introductory paintball rifle credits can buy."

A paintball rifle. My fingers relax slightly. "What happened to the bow? And suction-cup arrows?"

"Back in the toy chest. You've outgrown them."

"After one session?"

"That was all you needed. Plus, the arsenal of every great

marksman consists of a variety of weapons. If we stuck with bows and arrows, you'd be an archer. Which, as we know, isn't your calling."

Ike sounds as excited as Dad does on Christmas morning, when he gives me the single gift he picked out without Mom's help. Because Dad's an accountant, those gifts are usually office supplies; I don't have much use for economy-size packs of staples and rubber bands, but he loves giving them, so I love getting them.

This is what I think of as I pat the rifle and say, "Awesome. Thanks."

"Don't thank me yet. See what it can do first."

"Here?" My fingers tighten again. "Now?"

"Can you think of a better place and time?"

Yes. The huge field of mannequins. My empty dorm room. The Kanteen dining hall, which is likely vacant since it's two in the afternoon and in between meal times. Anywhere at midnight tonight, when kids and staff members are sound asleep and out of firing range.

Just not here, at the Performance Pavilion. Or now, when my fellow first-year Troublemakers are meeting with their respective troublemaking groups.

"I don't know . . . they seem pretty serious down there."

We're in the staff viewing box, where Ike told me to meet him. He leans forward and peers through the window that overlooks the stage.

"Yammering. That's all they're doing. Older TMs are bragging about their troublemaking conquests to younger TMs." He turns back. "Big heads are notorious side effects of a Kilter education. Do yourself a favor and keep the ego in check."

That won't be a problem.

"Is that why you're up here instead of down there?" I ask. "Because you don't want to get caught up in that?"

I've wondered about Ike's separation from older Troublemakers before. He participated in the tutor assignment performance but didn't hang around for the end of the ceremony. He wears a black ski parka instead of the silver one other Troublemakers wear. A patch is sewn on the left sleeve, but it's blank; there's no "KA" or group emblem. And while my classmates all received parkas at the ceremony, I didn't. Not that I'm complaining—I don't deserve any of the benefits I've received so far. But I do wonder why.

"I'm up here instead of down there because I'm not like them." He pauses. "And neither are you."

My eyes widen. Does that mean he . . . ? Like me, did he . . . ?

"Technically, we're members of the Sniper Squad," he says. "That's the group of TMs who use physical weapons to make trouble. Each member is master of one specific weapon—except me. I'm master of them all. And by the time we're done, you will be too."

That answers that. Unless Ike's used his skills to do something Annika doesn't know about, I'm still Kilter's only murderer.

"Shall we get started?" he asks.

Not wanting to be spotted, I've been sitting with my back to the low wall since arriving twenty minutes ago. Now I climb to my knees and turn around so that I'm facing the window. I rise up just enough to see through the glass. The groups are spread across the stage; the younger Troublemakers listen attentively to the older Troublemakers. Every now and then there's laughter and clapping.

Ike nudges me. Motions for me to hold out my hand. I do, and he drops five silver beads into my open palm.

"These don't look like paintballs," I whisper. They're small and heavy and resemble bullets.

"Metal casing," Ike whispers back. "For speed. It disintegrates upon firing. The actual ball's made of foam."

I must look skeptical, because he sits back on his heels. Unzips his parka. Pats his chest.

"Go ahead. Give me your best shot."

My eyes lift to his. "What?"

"You don't believe the balls are made of foam. You're worried you'll hurt someone. And I'm going to prove that you won't."

"But you're two feet away."

"Exactly. If I don't bleed, no one down there will."

This makes sense but still seems like a bad idea. "Can't I shoot your foot? Or maybe your—"

"All or nothing, Seamus. Anything in between is pointless."

He sounds so confident I take the gun from the sheath and drop the five beads into the slot labeled AMMO. I lift the gun, aim for his chest, and close my eyes. "Don't say I didn't offer."

There's a dull *thwat*. I open my eyes—and almost fall over.

Because Ike was wrong. He's bleeding. The bullet hit his chest and now dark red liquid spreads across his T-shirt.

"It's paint," he reminds me as I start to reach for him. He nods to the floor, where jagged silver chunks lie between us.

I stop reaching, and frown. "You couldn't have picked a different color?"

"This one's easy to see. And it freaks people out before they realize it's not blood." He returns to his knees next to me. "Each body part's worth a different number of demerits. Arms and legs are five, hands and feet ten, chest and back fifteen. Head's twenty. Your total goal's a hundred. Got it?"

"Yes. But what about the window?"

I don't know how he couldn't have thought of this, but I'm hopeful anyway. It's kind of hard to hit any target with any weapon when there's a plate of glass in the way.

My hope is short-lived. Because Ike presses a button on the low wall. And the window slides into the concrete.

"Anything else?" he asks.

There isn't—at least not that will get me out of this situation.

"Good," Ike says. "Now let's have some fun."

Taking a deep breath, I lift the gun. Close one eye. Press my pointer finger to the trigger. And pull.

Thwat.

The paintball hits the back of Chris Fisher, a fellow first-year in the Dramatists group. He shoots forward from the force and twists in his seat to try to see where he was struck. But the angle's too awkward. He doesn't see the red paint splattered across his coat. The paintball bounces silently under his chair, out of sight. A moment later he faces forward, puzzled but clearly not hurt.

I grin. Ike pats my shoulder.

"Fifteen demerits," he says. "Eighty-five to go."

I raise the gun and choose another target. The girls make me think of Miss Parsippany, so they're off-limits. That leaves the guys, who are far enough away that I can pretend they're Bartholomew John and Alex Ortiz.

I pick one of the Biohazards. The older Troublemakers in that group are having some sort of burping-contest reenactment, which has the younger Troublemakers in hysterics. Hoping he's so distracted he won't feel a thing, I point and shoot at a kid in the back row.

Thwat.

The ball skims his shoulder. As the red paint spreads, he doesn't even blink.

"Awesome," I whisper.

"Twenty," Ike whispers. "Eighty to go."

I keep shooting. At first I worry only about making contact, not about aiming for specific body parts. I miss a few times, but soon I'm getting hit after hit. Ike gives me more ammo, and I reload. Feeling more comfortable, I focus on the leg of my next target. The hand of the one after that. To keep alarm at a minimum, I don't hit the same group twice in a row. I also concentrate on the younger Troublemakers, figuring they're less likely to speak up and interrupt the older ones they want to impress.

Before I know it, I'm out of ammo again. I smile at Ike and hold out one hand.

"This just might be the coolest present I've ever gotten," I say.

"I know." He smiles back and drops more paintballs in my open palm.

Unfortunately, my good aim—or luck—doesn't last. I've just fired my seventh shot when my target sneezes. His head falls forward . . . and the paintball hits the chest of his group leader.

"Another fifteen," Ike hisses. "Good job. Now run!"

He leaps to his feet. Down below, the older Troublemaker I hit looks at the paint on his chest. The startling image silences his group—but only briefly. They follow their leader's lead and are soon on their feet, scanning the pavilion. Troublemakers in other groups notice the commotion. It doesn't take long for my formerly silent targets to speak up and for every person in the arena to scatter in search of the culprit.

I spin around to ask Ike what we do now, but he's already gone. Still holding the gun, I scramble to my feet and lunge for the extra ammunition, Ike's duffel bag, my backpack. It's a lot to carry, and my palms are slick with sweat. I try to readjust as I start for the steps leading to the viewing-box door, but it's too much. The gun slips from my grasp. A paintball fires straight up, ricochets off an overhead lamp, and disappears on the other side of the low wall.

A second later, there's a scream.

I freeze.

"Didn't see that one coming!" a familiar voice calls out from below.

I force my feet to move, then peer over the wall. Only one person remains on the pavilion stage: Wyatt. Our art teacher. He wasn't part of the tutor-trainee gathering and carries an easel and paint box, like he just came to do some work.

A beet-red splotch spreads across his abdomen. He gives the entire arena a thumbs-up, then proceeds to arrange his easel and materials like nothing happened.

I step back, relieved he's okay but worried I've just wasted valuable time. Troublemakers are on the move. They'll be up here any second. If I flee now, chances are slim I'll make it out without running into them—and I'm too nervous to lie about where I've been. I could stay and hide under the seats . . . but if they find me, won't that be worse than if I just came clean?

"GS Four en route."

I stop and listen to the noises coming from the hallway. There's muffled static as the Good Samaritan uses his walkie-talkie.

"On first mezzanine. No sign of subject—yet."

His voice is louder. He's coming closer.

"Open up!"

Loud, sharp pounding shakes the viewing-box walls. I brace for the door to fly open . . . but it doesn't. There's a slam and more muffled static as the Good Samaritan enters another room down the hall.

Without thinking, I grab the gun from the floor. Turn it around so the barrel's aimed at me. And fire.

Once. Twice. Three times.

Paintballs hit my foot. My shin. My thigh.

"Not bad."

I jump. The viewing-box door's wide open. And I'm not alone.

"Shooting yourself so you look like a victim and not the attacker. Annika would be proud."

I open my mouth to try to explain, apologize, say *anything* that will make this seem better than it is.

But before I can find the words, Elinor's eyes lock on mine.

And then she leaves.

Chapter 13

DEMERITS: 750
GOLD STARS: 60

Hoodlum Hotline, how may I direct your call?"

"I'd like to report a theft, please."

"Proceed."

I scoot farther back in the closet, behind Lemon's ski parka. "Aaron Potts stole a bag of pretzels from Matilda Jackson. Today, outside the Kanteen."

The clicking on the other end of the line stops. "A bag of pretzels?"

"Yes."

"And you think this is worth reporting because . . . ?"

"Matilda Jackson loves pretzels," I say. "They're all she eats."

I actually have no idea how Matilda Jackson feels about pretzels, but this gets the operator typing again.

"Did you witness this theft firsthand?" she asks.

"Yes."

"Seamus Hinkle, tattling in the third degree!"

The line goes dead. I wait a minute, then dial again.

"Hoodlum Hotline, how may I direct your call?"

"I'd like to call my parents, please."

"Sorry, no family phone calls. You can tell them how much fun you're having on Parents' Day."

"Okay," I say. "Thanks."

"Seamus Hinkle, Parental Communication Attempt!"

Click.

I wait another minute. Dial again.

"Hoodlum Hotline, how may I— Wait. Is this Seamus Hinkle?"

"Yes?"

"You do realize you rack up gold stars each time we talk, right?"

I do. That's the point. But I don't want her to know that.

"This is the last time," I say. "For something I just can't let slide. Call me old-fashioned."

"All righty, old-fashioned. Let's hear it."

"Brian Benson programmed every TV in the first-year dorm to *Rocky and Bullwinkle*. We can't change the channel."

She stops typing. "And?"

I pause. "Have you seen *Rocky and Bullwinkle*? The news would be more entertaining."

The typing resumes. "It's called a classic, but I suppose that's beside the point. Anything else I can help you with today?"

"Nope."

"You sure? You're not going to call me again in five seconds? Because we can bang out all your reports right now. Save me the trouble of answering the phone—and stopping my word searches midsearch."

"I'm sure."

"Okeydoke. Seamus Hinkle, tattling in the fourth degree!"

Click.

I put down the phone and pick up my K-Pak, which buzzes with a new message.

TO: shinkle@kilteracademy.org
FROM: kommissary@kilteracademy.org
SUBJECT: Don't Stop Now!

Congratulations, Seamus! You recently earned hundreds of demerits—and credits—for getting a bunch of teachers, unleashing the wrath of the Kilter Painter 1000, and completing assignments. And you know what that means. Shopping spree at the Kommissary!

If you want to really load up, though, you might want to disconnect your phone. Two minutes ago, with 750 demerits, 60 gold stars, and only one previous purchase (the Kilter Pocket Extinguisher, cost: 20 credits), you had 670 credits and could've bought the stainless steel Kilter Mug Guard (650 credits), which every serious Sniper Squad member should eventually call his own.

I click on the flashing camera. A shiny silver face shield, which looks like something an ice-hockey goalie would wear, appears.

But after your latest phone activity, you can now only afford the plastic Kilter Mug Guard (600 credits), which is fine for ordinary Troublemakers—but not extraordinary ones. You should be as protected as possible!

Maybe you fell asleep with your nose pressed to the redial button? If so . . . WAKE UP! ☺

At Your Service,

The Kommissary Krew

I exit my e-mail and load the Kilter Report Kard. When it updates, I see I've just earned sixty gold stars. That's barely a dent in all the demerits I've accumulated, but it's a start.

Because here's the thing. I can't change the fact that Annika and the teachers think I'm some sort of natural-born Troublemaker, because I can't change the fact that I killed Miss Parsippany. Plus, considering how much trouble I've made since arriving here, intentional or not, they might be onto something. But as far as I can tell, the verdict's still out with my fellow Troublemakers. Which means that if I can just earn enough gold stars to balance out the demerits, maybe they'll eventually decide

I'm no different from any of them. Right now our demerits and gold stars aren't public knowledge, but that could change at any point. And who knows? This is a school for professional Troublemakers. If someone wants to know how well a classmate is doing, I'm sure they can find out. At the very least, I won't raise suspicions by checking into the Kommissary with a million credits.

I feel pretty good about my progress until my eyes fall to the bottom of the list. Then blood drains from my face like sand through the hourglass in the opening of Mom's favorite soap opera.

CURRENT CLASS RANKING: 4 OUT OF 31

Fourth. I've had a month less to make trouble . . . and I'm *fourth*. That means I'm ahead of 75 percent of my class. It also means I have, like, a million more gold stars to earn.

I debate calling the Hoodlum Hotline again with another Parental Communication Attempt. Before I can decide, I hear a door open and close, and people talking in our room.

I'd told Lemon I was going into the closet to watch a movie on my K-Pak in total darkness. So I toss the phone in my sweatshirt hood, where I'd hidden it before telling that little white lie, and open the closet door.

"Dude, I'm serious. It's the only way. If we all—"

Abe's back is to me. He stops talking when Lemon looks past him, and then turns around. Seeing me, he frowns.

"Short movie?" Lemon asks.

"Bad movie," I say. Since I was only in the closet for fifteen minutes.

"Bummer," he says.

I stand there, not sure what to do. Abe's blocking my desk chair. Gabby's sitting on my bed. I could go into the bathroom, but I've already showered and don't want them to think I'm doing anything else in there that takes longer than thirty seconds to finish. As far as I know, word hasn't gotten out about my post-burrito library performance, but I'm not adding any more fuel to that fire, just in case.

"Abe wants to form an alliance."

"Dude." Abe throws his hands in the air.

Lemon ignores him and flops on his bed. "He thinks it's the only way to get Mystery."

"Mystery?" I say.

"Mr. History," Gabby says. "Also known as Mr. Tempest."

"I thought Houdini said we didn't have to get him," I say.

"Average Troublemakers don't," Abe says. "*I* do. I want that extra credit, whatever it is."

"Abe just launched an epic spray-paint attack on him," Gabby adds.

"And was defeated before the first drops hit their target," Lemon says.

"Really?" Abe puts his hands on his hips. "You *really* want to involve the new kid?"

"Relax," Lemon says. "Hinkle's cool."

"*Hinkle* started late. *Hinkle* gets special treatment. *Hinkle* is so loved by Annika and our teachers, he's practically one of them." Abe looks at Lemon. "How do you know he can be trusted?"

Lemon looks at me. "I just do."

This is followed by a long, awkward pause.

"That's it?" Abe asks.

"That's it," Lemon says.

Abe half sighs, half groans. "Fine. Whatever. But even if he *can* be trusted—which I doubt—he's still a month behind. You and I aren't exactly buddies, but I came to you because I know you're at the top of the class. I know this because I'm second and Gabby's third, and you're the only other Troublemaker who's gotten every other teacher."

I watch Lemon's expression. It doesn't change.

"If we work together," Abe says, "I know we can beat Mystery. Probably faster and easier than any Troublemaker before."

"Don't you want to be the best?" Gabby asks. "I mean, look at everything we've gotten just by being here. Imagine what we might get by being better than the rest."

"Like rewards?" Lemon asks. "Prizes?"

"The Kilter Smoke Detector with Automatic Flame Eliminator?" Abe says.

Lemon sits up. Fast.

"Three Troublemakers can make three times as much trouble—and get what they want three times as fast." Abe lifts his chin toward the smoke-stained ceiling. "That kind of speed might come in handy."

Lemon's furry eyebrows lower. He eyes the trash can in the middle of the floor. We took turns scrubbing it after last night's fire, but no amount of cleaning will turn the blackened metal silver again.

"Fine," Lemon finally says, sitting back.

Abe whoops. Gabby squeals.

"On one condition," Lemon adds.

"Name it." Abe smiles.

"Hinkle's in too."

Abe's smile falls. "What? No way."

"That's okay," I say quickly. "I mean, thanks, Lemon. That's really nice of you, but—"

"Hinkle's in, or I'm out." Lemon's voice is firm. "And you're right. I'm first in the class. I have been for weeks, even after being docked four days of troublemaking by the Good Samaritans. If you're serious about beating Mystery, you'll accept these terms. If you're not, I'm sure I can get him on my own."

Abe steps toward Lemon and lowers his voice like I'm not standing three feet away. "But he's a *month* behind," he says. "He'll be deadweight."

Deadweight. I almost laugh.

"He probably hasn't gotten any teachers besides Fern yet," Abe continues, practically whispering.

"Hinkle," Lemon says, "how many teachers have you taken down so far?"

I swallow, embarrassed to admit it even though I know it'll be considered a good thing. "Five."

Abe spins around. Gabby gasps.

"Five?" she says.

"Which ones?" Abe asks, suspicious.

"Fern, Samara, Wyatt, Lizzie, and Houdini." All accidentally—including Houdini, who didn't notice when his sunglasses fell off his head and into my backpack after math last week. And Lizzie, our language arts teacher, who was caught off guard and had no idea what I was saying when I tried talking to her with a mouthful of fish sticks at lunch the other day. But I leave that part out.

"That leaves Devin—"

"And Mystery," Lemon finishes, cutting Abe off.

Abe stares at me, then shakes his head and turns back to Lemon. "Still. He's a month behind on classes and assignments. We know things he doesn't. There's no way he'll be able to keep up."

"Hinkle," Lemon says, "how many demerits do you have right now?"

"Seven hundred and fifty." Less the sixty gold stars I already had and the sixty I just earned in the closet, but I leave that out also.

Abe's mouth drops open. So does Gabby's. And for just a second, I'm proud.

"What about Annika?" he tries next, his voice thin with

frustration. "And the rest of the staff? For whatever reason, they love him—and will probably be paying close attention to him. If he's in the alliance, they'll pay close attention to *us*. It'll be way harder to take down Mystery if they're watching our every move."

"They already watch our every move." Lemon sits up. Leans toward Abe. "And have you stopped to consider *why* Annika and the staff love him?"

Abe starts to speak—then stops.

"They let him start late," Lemon says patiently, like he's talking to a five-year-old. "He's already almost caught up. This is a school for Troublemakers." He pauses. "Think about it."

As Abe thinks, my heart races. My breath quickens. I lean against the dresser just in case they ask me something that makes my knees give out.

"How about a compromise?" Gabby asks a minute later.

Lemon leans to the side and peers around Abe. "What kind?"

"A test. If Seamus passes, he's in. If he doesn't, he's not."

"That sounds fair." Abe releases a sigh of relief, apparently confident that whatever the test is, I won't pass.

Lemon nods slowly, then looks at me. "What do you think?"

"Let's do it," I say.

They huddle together. I sit at the foot of my bed and wait, as certain of the outcome as Abe seems to be. It was great of Lemon to fight for me, but I don't need to be in the alliance. I don't need to get Mystery. I just need to get through the semester so I can go home. Abe reminds me a little of Bartholomew John, but proving him wrong isn't more important than sliding by—as under the radar as possible.

Three minutes later, the huddle breaks.

"Okay," Gabby says, rubbing her palms together. "Prepare to stare."

"I'm sorry," I say. "What?"

"A staring contest," Lemon says. "You versus Gabby."

"In the interest of full disclosure—and fairness—you should know I'm good." Gabby brings over a desk chair, places it in front of me, and sits. "*Really* good."

This doesn't seem like a very serious challenge to me, but it's immediately clear that to Gabby, it's as serious as challenges get. She rubs her eyes. Opens them. Closes them. Three times slowly, then five times fast. Without moving her head, she looks all the way to the right, then all the way to the left. Up, then down. She places her thumbs just below her bottom lashes and her pointer fingers above her top lashes, and stretches her skin until her blue eyes look like they'll fall out of their sockets.

And then she cracks her knuckles.

"Ready?" she asks.

"Sure," I say.

"Five seconds," Abe announces. "Four . . . three . . . two . . . one . . . go!"

Her eyes lock on mine. They're intense. I almost expect laser beams to shoot out from her pupils.

Her focus is so uncomfortable I'm ready to forfeit ten seconds in. And I would . . . but then Abe sneezes. Once. Twice. Three times. The last is followed by a soft *thump*, which I'm pretty sure is Lemon's fist connecting with Abe's shoulder, since the sneezes stop after that.

I know instantly that he's trying to rattle me. Just like Bartholomew John on Fish Stick Tuesdays. So I open my eyes wider. Pretend Gabby's are on a TV screen, that I'm playing a video game and this is the last, most difficult level.

Three minutes and eleven seconds later, Gabby blinks.

I win.

And Abe reluctantly accepts me into the alliance.

"Impressive," Lemon says after they've left. He hands me a wet washcloth. "Beating the master starer at her own game."

I thank him and press the washcloth to my closed, dry eyes. I'm glad I can't see his face when I speak again.

"By the way, what you said to Abe about why Annika and the staff love me . . ." I take a deep breath, count my pounding heartbeats. "Do *you* know?"

"How would I? You haven't told me."

"I know. But I just thought . . . that maybe you heard . . . or maybe someone else said . . . ?"

"Seamus," Lemon says, "whatever it is, don't sweat it. We all have our stuff. Trust me."

Chapter 14

DEMERITS: 760
GOLD STARS: 120

For its purposes, the alliance couldn't have formed at a better time. Because the next morning we wake to K-Pak messages instructing us to pick up bagged breakfasts and be at the front gate by nine o'clock. Lemon and I walk together and meet up with Abe and Gabby on the way. A golf cart pulls up at nine sharp; it looks like the one I rode in with Ike, except it's as long as a school bus and has thirty seats instead of two.

And who's sitting behind the wheel? The Mystery man

himself. Sitting next to him, so busy on her K-Pak she doesn't look up, is Annika.

"Good morning," says Alison Parker, an expert knock-knock joker, as she steps on board.

"Hello, Annika," says Eric Fisher, a talented hide-and-seeker. "Mr. Tempest."

"Yo," says Abe.

This last greeting makes me cringe, but it gets the same response the other, more polite greetings do: a quick smile from Annika and silence from Mr. Tempest. Our history teacher, wearing a long, black wool coat, black gloves, and dark sunglasses, says nothing. Does nothing. As we fill the golf cart, he simply sits still and looks straight ahead.

As soon as we're seated, both Lemon's and my K-Paks buzz.

TO: loliver@kilteracademy.org;
shinkle@kilteracademy.org;
gryan@kilteracademy.org
FROM: ahansen@kilteracademy.org
SUBJECT: !!!

Amazing timing! Need to strategize, but too many ears here. Let's brainstorm on our own now and discuss once we get wherever we're going.

—Abe

He must really be concerned about eavesdroppers, because he and Gabby are sitting right in front of us.

My K-Pak buzzes again.

TO: ahansen@kilteracademy.org;
shinkle@kilteracademy.org;
gryan@kilteracademy.org
FROM: loliver@kilteracademy.org
SUBJECT: Chill

The message box is blank.

"You might want to resend," I tell Lemon. "The message is missing."

He looks at the open note on my K-Pak screen. "Nope. It's not."

Okay. Lemon wants us to chill. I put away my K-Pak and sit back.

"Have you had class with Mr. Tempest before?" I whisper.

"Once," Lemon says quietly. "It was the shortest lecture ever. He told us how Annika started the school twenty years ago, when she was eighteen. She was the only teacher—and chef and custodian and everything else—but she did such a good job, she was able to hire new teachers and expand the program right away. He also said that she thinks the reason Kilter's been so successful since then is because she has really high hiring standards."

"Which are?"

"Extraordinary troublemaking talent, of course, and kidlike mentality."

"How can she tell how kidlike someone is?" I ask.

"By their age. Apparently, if you're a day over twenty-five, you're fine to flip burgers in the Kanteen . . . but you're too old to teach."

"But—"

The golf cart takes off with a jolt, stopping me from pointing out that Mr. Tempest, whose wrinkles and thin white hair suggest that twenty-five came and went a long time ago, doesn't exactly meet those standards.

We veer away from the main entrance. The cart travels so fast the scenery flies by in green, blue, and brown streaks, making it impossible to tell what we pass. Clear panes of glass slide up the cart's sides like windows, blocking out potentially revealing sounds and smells. The only clues come when the cart shoots up or down or swings from side to side, which suggests we're traveling across mountainous terrain.

The motion makes my stomach turn, and ten minutes into the trip I have to look away. I can't move my head because of the force pushing it back into the seat, but I can roll my eyes, so I focus on the still figures and objects inside the cart. Next to me, Lemon's eyes are closed. In front of us, Gabby's head is turned permanently to the right as she chatters away with—or more accurately, *at*—Abe, who uses both hands to keep the graphic novel he's reading from colliding with his face.

We shoot to the right. I grab my bagged breakfast to keep it from falling off my lap, and the smell of eggs, cheese, and fish sticks wafts toward my nose. The normally pleasant odor combined with the cart's swerving makes my stomach churn faster. I force my head to the left and lift my hand to the glass next to me. I'm about to push to see if it'll give in the event of a hurling emergency when I catch a flash of red.

Elinor. I didn't see her board, but she must be sitting somewhere nearby; when the cart tilts to the left and the sun shines in from the right, I can see her hair reflected in the glass.

I keep my eyes fixed on that one spot, and soon my stomach settles. By the time we come to an abrupt stop half an hour later, I even feel hungry enough to take a big bite of my egg-and-fish bagel.

"You might want to save your breakfasts," Mr. Tempest calls back as the glass slides down the sides of the cart. "It may be a long time until your next meal."

"It's zero degrees out there," Gabby says with a shiver.

This might be a slight exaggeration, but it's definitely colder wherever we are than it was back at Kilter. I'm wearing jeans and a fleece and am still instantly chilled as I step outside. Rubbing my arms, I look around at the leafless trees, gray sky, and frost-covered ground. We appear to be in a clearing in the middle of the woods—somewhere near the Arctic Circle.

"There are hats, gloves, and hiking shoes for each of you," Mr. Tempest says once we're all outside. He aims his K-Pak at the bottom of the cart and a cargo space opens; it resembles a large dresser drawer and is stuffed with gear.

"Hiking shoes?" Gabby says. "I thought we had history this morning—not gym."

"You do have history." Mr. Tempest takes a black wool cap from his coat pocket and puts it on. The pom-pom on top quivers in the bitter wind. "And if you do well, you just might make some too."

If anyone besides me wonders what this means, they're too cold to care. We all find our cold-weather accessories and bundle up quickly.

"As I mentioned in our last meeting," Mr. Tempest continues, "over the next few weeks I'll be telling you all you need to know about Kilter Academy's illustrious yet top secret past. Before we begin today, you should know one very important thing." He taps his head with one crooked finger. "What's under here? Weakens with age and without use. That's why your parents sometimes ask you if you've finished your homework two minutes after they asked the first time."

He shoots Annika, who stands off to the side and appears to be listening attentively, a wary look.

"And why they pack broccoli in my lunch after I've told them a thousand times that I hate broccoli?" a tall girl named Jillian asks.

He slowly lowers his head and peers at her over the top of

his sunglasses, which don't really seem necessary since the sun is hidden by fat gray clouds. Annika clears her throat a second later, and he lifts his head and addresses us again.

"The more you train your brain, the better you'll be at remembering things adults often don't but should. Keen attention to detail and a sharp memory are two of the most important assets a Troublemaker can have. They'll serve you well in nearly every scenario—including this one."

"Which is what, exactly?" Lemon asks.

Mr. Tempest frowns. "Follow me and find out."

He turns and starts across the clearing. Annika hurries several feet ahead of him. A few kids look back at the cart wistfully. I don't blame them—the windows are still down, but there must be some lingering warmth inside. Plus, if Kilter's in the middle of nowhere, where we are now is an isolated, uninhabited island completely off the map of nowhere. The cart might not be a car, but it can still take us back to some sort of civilization.

"Hinkle!"

I spin around. Lemon lopes after Mr. Tempest, Gabby runs to keep up with Lemon's long strides, and Abe waves to me as he hurries after them all.

I follow them, and other kids follow me. I look over my shoulder halfway across the clearing and see Elinor lagging far behind. She keeps her eyes lowered and stops every few feet to squat and examine something on the ground. Thinking she might be nervous, I slow down to wait for her—but then someone grabs my hood and yanks me back.

"Hustle, Hinkle," Abe says.

I glance behind me once more before picking up the pace. At the edge of the clearing we enter a narrow trail that starts out flat but steepens almost immediately. It's covered in dead branches and loose rocks, which the thick, ridged soles of the hiking shoes grip better than my sneakers could. The temperature drops as we climb; when we reach a second clearing twenty minutes later, snowflakes are falling.

"Rest stop," Mr. Tempest says. He leans against the clearing's lone, dead tree, removes a water bottle from his coat pocket, and drinks. For an older guy, he must be in pretty good shape. He's breathing quickly—but not as quickly as some of my classmates.

"You mean we're not there yet?" Gabby gasps, collapsing to the ground. She shares the bad news with our classmates as they emerge from the trail. Many groan and whine, but all eventually follow Mr. Tempest's lead and take water bottles from their bagged breakfasts.

I drink and look around. Annika's already started up another trail. Elinor enters the clearing last, just as Mr. Tempest starts walking again. While the rest of the alliance starts after him, I jog over to her.

"This was just a rest stop," I explain.

She's wearing her parka hood, which is rimmed in fake white fur. When she looks up, she reminds me of an Arctic Circle snow bunny. "Oh," she says.

"Yeah. So." Despite the cold and snow, I'm suddenly warm. "You should probably drink some water."

"I'll keep that in mind."

This isn't the answer I'm expecting. I have no idea what to say next.

"You were looking out for me," she says a moment later.

I shake my head. The heat in my cheeks intensifies. "I was looking out for everyone. You know—leave no man behind and all that."

"Who's looking out for *you*, Seamus?" she asks. Then, "Your boys are gone."

I look behind us. The only other person in the clearing is a quiet, chubby Troublemaker named Marcus. He sits on a rock, eating a sandwich.

"Go ahead," Elinor says. "We'll be fine."

I turn back, and our eyes meet. Hers are clear, steady. They make me believe her.

It doesn't take long to catch up with the rest of the class. I weave through the stragglers and rejoin Lemon, Gabby, and Abe at the front of the pack. The farther we go, the happier I am to have listened to Elinor, because if I'd waited five more minutes I never would've found them. There are countless trails up here, and as soon as we take one we turn off onto another. They twist and wind, cutting through a million identical dead trees and throwing off any sense of direction. When we finally enter a third clearing, I have no idea how long it took us to get there.

"Holy horror movie," Abe says.

It's an accurate response. Because unlike the first two, this clearing isn't empty. There's a carousel. A Ferris wheel. A spinning swing set. A small roller coaster. Game booths and concession stands are scattered between the rides.

Only no one's screaming from the roller coaster. No one's

shooting hoops for cheap stuffed animals or eating funnel cakes with powdered sugar. Judging by the rusty rails, peeling paint, and rotting booths, no one's done any of those things in a very, very long time.

Mr. Tempest opens his arms wide.

"Welcome," he says, "to Annika's Apex."

Chapter 15

DEMERITS: 760
GOLD STARS: 120

Doesn't he mean Annika's *Asylum*?" Abe whispers to Lemon.

Lemon doesn't answer. He surveys the deteriorating amusement park, then turns his attention to Mr. Tempest. Mr. Tempest waits for everyone—including Elinor and Marcus, who have made remarkable time—to come into the clearing and gather around him before continuing.

"Thanks to shrewd investing, Annika's father, Maximus Kilter, was a very wealthy man. Annika grew up in a sprawling stone estate not far from the academy grounds and spent holidays at other sprawling estates in Georgia, Montana, and California. She received whatever she wanted, including puppies, ponies, and more porcelain dolls than the world's biggest toy store could ever sell."

Mr. Tempest leads us to the park's entrance, which is marked by a crooked iron arch. At the top of the arch, "Annika's Apex" is spelled out in loopy, curly letters and surrounded by elaborate iron flowers. Annika herself stands off to the side, her face blank, listening but not contributing.

"Before each birthday," Mr. Tempest continues, "Maximus would ask Annika to name the one thing she absolutely couldn't spend the next year without. For her sixth birthday, Annika's answer was Candy Land."

"The board game?" Abe asks.

"Yes. Her nanny's daughter had brought it over one afternoon, and the girls played together for hours. After that, Annika wanted her own."

"That seems like a pretty modest request," Lemon says.

"It was," Mr. Tempest agrees. "Perhaps too much so, because on the morning she woke up six years old, her father took her for a ride and presented her with this—her very own real-life Candy Land."

He aims his K-Pak at the side of a dilapidated concession stand. A moving image of a tall man and a little girl in pink pajamas appears. Their backs are to the camera. As we watch, Maximus takes Annika's hand and brings her before the arch, which is wrapped in a big white bow. She unwraps the bow and they head inside the park, which is bright and loud and filled with kids. The sky is blue and the treetops are thick and green.

At one point, Annika's Apex looked like the happiest place on earth.

"What about the board game?" Marcus looks at Annika. "Did you get that, too?"

Annika looks at Mr. Tempest. The concession stand wall goes dark.

"No," Mr. Tempest says. "Annika did not get the board game."

"But that was what you—she—really wanted," Jillian says. "Her dad didn't listen to her."

"He listened," Mr. Tempest says, sounding almost sad. "He just didn't hear."

We follow him through the arch. The snow falls faster now, covering the rides and structures in a thin white blanket. It might look almost pretty, like something you'd see in an old picture, if not for the broken lightbulbs and exposed nails poking through the snow. Between them and the silence, it's hard to believe this is the same place we just saw in the video. Thinking it must be hard for her to see her childhood playground like this, I sneak a peek at Annika . . . but she hurries ahead of us and ducks behind a candy-apple booth.

"So what happened?" Lemon asks. "Did Annika get tired of the park? Is that why it looks like this?"

Mr. Tempest stops by the carousel and stands before a fake black horse adorned in chipped red flowers. "She didn't have a chance to get tired of it. Her father was called away on business the next day and was gone for months. He promised to bring her back upon his return, but then he was always busy with meetings, phone calls, and eventually, more business trips."

"What about her mother?" I ask. "Couldn't she bring Annika?"

Mr. Tempest looks down, seems to study the snow at his feet, and then looks up again. "Lucelia Kilter . . . wasn't well. She was too weak to do what most mothers her age could, and her condition only worsened after Annika's sister was born."

"Annika has a sister?" Gabby asks. "Does she work for the academy too?"

Mr. Tempest pauses.

"Wait," Abe says. "You mean Annika was here only once? On the morning of her sixth birthday?"

"Sadly, yes," Mr. Tempest says.

It's hard to feel bad for Annika when her dad went to the trouble of building her her very own amusement park—even if she did enjoy it only one time. But I still do.

"Chin up, Troublemakers!" Annika declares suddenly, zipping out from behind the candy-apple booth on a supersleek silver scooter. She does a few figure eights, sending snow flying into the air, and then stops before us. "Who here brought their bicycles with them to the academy?"

No one answers.

She tries again. "Who *wishes* they'd brought their bicycles with them to the academy?"

A few hands appear.

"Who wishes that instead of their bicycles they had state-of-the-art, voice-operated, Kilter Series 7000 scooters that could get them from their dorms to the Kanteen in ten seconds?"

Thirty-one hands appear, mine included.

"That's what I thought." Annika hops off the scooter. "The first student to complete Mr. Tempest's history task with ten demerits will ride this baby into the sunset—or to dinner, as the case may be."

"What task?" Abe asks.

"The one in which I find out how well you've been paying attention this morning," our teacher says.

I try to recall everything I've learned. The first thing that comes to mind is that history is supposed to help train our brains. Guessing we're seconds away from a pop quiz, I frantically try to remember what I just learned about Annika. Her father's name was Maximilian, she had a lot of Barbie dolls, she wanted Chutes and Ladders on her fifth birthday but instead she got . . .

My thoughts keep going, but I no longer hear them. A weird whirring noise that sounds like an enormous lawn mower capable of cutting all the grass in New York in a single push grows louder, comes closer.

And a silver helicopter appears over the tree line.

"Here's our ride!" Mr. Tempest shouts. "If you want yours, be the first one back down the mountain!"

"You're *leaving*?" Gabby yells.

The helicopter swoops toward us. The wind from the whipping blades pushes us back, forces our arms over our heads. A metal ladder falls from the open helicopter door. Annika climbs it easily, and Mr. Tempest follows close behind.

"I'll be watching from above!" he shouts. "If you get into trouble, I'll know!"

To me, getting into trouble in the woods means getting lost. Crossing a protective mama bear and her cubs. Being so hungry you eat the pretty red berries you know are poisonous but hope will give you enough energy to find the nearest emergency room.

But I'm pretty sure Mr. Tempest's referring to a completely different kind of trouble.

There's a tug on my hood. I spin around to see Lemon jogging, head lowered, toward the iron arch. Gabby's a few feet behind him, and Abe's a few feet behind her. Abe waves for me to follow.

"Shouldn't we all stick together?" Jillian shouts. "For, like, safety in numbers?"

"Don't you want to win that scooter?" Eric hollers.

"Not more than I want to stay alive!"

For a second, the group's torn and I'm relieved. There *is* safety in numbers—and control, too. If we stick together and refuse to participate in the task, Annika and Mr. Tempest will have no choice but to cancel it and send helicopters for the rest of us. They wouldn't let us freeze to death up here.

Or maybe they would. Because the helicopter, with them inside, has already disappeared back over the tree line.

"It's too quiet," Marcus says when the air stills.

"This place is kind of scary," Jillian adds.

"I'm out of here," Eric says.

With that, kids start running. I do too. We stay in a loose clump until we reach the woods, and then we're forced apart by rocks, fallen branches, and a dozen different trail entrances. The paths all look the same, and everyone has a different idea of which one led us to the top of the mountain. I'm scanning the snow for fresh footprints when something small and hard hits the top of my head—and a pebble lands at my feet. I look up to see Lemon, Gabby, and Abe perched in the limbs of a tall, leafless tree.

Well, Lemon and Abe are perched. Gabby's arms and legs are wrapped so tightly around the tree trunk I wouldn't be surprised if it snapped in two.

My allegiance to the alliance isn't particularly strong, but with everyone else scattering, a group of four seems to be the biggest—and safest—I'm going to get. Plus, Lemon's fire-starting skills will come in handy when the sun finally sets over this icy tundra. They don't seem to want to share their location, so I wait for a cluster of classmates to pass by before turning toward the tree. Plenty of grooves for my fingers and toes make for a fairly easy climb.

"Way to keep up," Abe hisses when I reach the branch beneath his.

"Sorry," I whisper.

"Relax," Lemon says. "Look."

We do. The elevation gives us a good view of this part of the mountain—including the trails. We can see where they lead and which ones our classmates have taken. To our right, Elinor and Marcus move slowly down a longer, twisty trail. Elinor holds out her hand every few feet to help her partner across slippery patches. Our other classmates fill the paths to our left.

"Hudson, Taylor, and Brown." Abe nods to a trio of Troublemakers taking the lead. "They're the fastest—and our biggest competition."

"Are they?" Lemon asks.

Abe looks at him. Lemon looks up. The silver helicopter hovers overhead, so far away you could mistake it for a bird.

"Besides Mystery, I mean." Abe's cheeks, already pink from the cold, darken to fuchsia. "Obviously."

"He's, like, ten thousand feet in the air," Gabby says. "Unless one of you has a secret flying talent you didn't tell the rest of us about, I think we're out of luck."

Lemon settles back against the branch. Crosses his arms over his chest. Waits.

"The golf cart," I say.

Abe's head snaps toward me. "What about it?"

"It's at the base of the mountain."

"And?"

"And it needs a driver." My eyes meet Lemon's. "You think we can get Mystery down there, after the helicopter lands."

Lemon's lips lift in the slightest hint of a smile. "I think we can try."

"Right," Abe says, like he was thinking this all along. "Of course. We'll need to book it, though, if we're going to beat everyone else to the punch."

He starts to shimmy down the branch. Gabby looks from Lemon to him and back to Lemon. Lemon stays put, so I do too.

"Hello?" Abe says when he reaches the trunk. "What are you waiting for?"

"You to share your plan," Lemon says. "For what we'll do when we're back down the mountain. You have one, right?"

Abe's cheeks darken from fuchsia to maroon. "Sure. We'll just . . . I think we should . . . we can definitely get him by . . ." His voice trails off as he searches the ground for clues.

"We need to stop them," I say, my pulse quickening. "The other Troublemakers. If we're all down there at the same time, Mystery will probably expect someone to try something and be on the lookout."

"Yes." Lemon sits up. "How?"

I can't tell if he asks because he doesn't know, or because he does and just wants us to figure it out for ourselves. He is first in the class, after all. He might've had this thought out before we even started climbing the mountain.

"Too bad we don't have another prize," Gabby says. "Something bigger and better than the scooter that we could lure them away with."

"That is too bad," Lemon says thoughtfully. "But then . . . they don't know that we don't."

He takes his K-Pak from his parka pocket and types quickly. When he's done, he holds it out so we can see the screen.

> ATTENTION, TROUBLEMAKERS! Today's challenge consists of two parts. You know the first. Here's the second:
>
> Three gold rings are hidden throughout the carousel in Annika's Apex. The first students to return to the top of the mountain and find them win a Kilter Series 9000 scooter with attached sidecar AND 500 demerits. This is your chance to leave your mark on Kilter's illustrious legacy—and win some fabulous prizes in the process!
>
> Regards,
>
> Mr. Tempest

"What would a Kilter Series 9000 scooter do that a 7000 doesn't?" Gabby asks. "Turn into a submarine underwater?"

"If we're lucky, that's what they'll want to find out," Lemon says.

"You're going to send that to everyone?" I ask. "What if they don't check their K-Paks in time?"

"I can't actually send it, because they'll see it came from my K-Mail address—not Mystery's."

"Then how are they going to get the message?" There's a twinge of satisfaction in Abe's voice, like he's pleased Lemon's plan won't work. We may be in an alliance, but he clearly wants to be leader.

"You all have your K-Paks?" Lemon asks.

We nod.

"I think you should copy this note so you each have it. Then we'll split up, run down the trails, and show it to our classmates. We'll need to make it seem like we just got it and wanted to make sure everyone else did too."

"Never going to work," Abe says.

"It will if you make the challenge—and the prize—sound like the most exciting one we've ever had," Lemon says. "Think you can do that, Hansen?"

Abe frowns. He doesn't want Lemon to be right, but he also

doesn't want to be the one to mess up the plan if there's a chance it might succeed.

"I can do it," Gabby says.

"Awesome." Lemon looks at me. "Seamus?"

"I'm in." Which is different from saying I can.

Lemon shifts his gaze to Abe. After a few more seconds of pouting, Abe sighs, sits up, and takes out his K-Pak.

"Fine," he says. "But if this doesn't work—"

"It's not your fault," Lemon finishes. "Understood."

Gabby and I take out our K-Paks. As we all copy Lemon's note, he talks us through the rest of the plan.

"Once everyone else starts back up, we'll continue down. If you get lost, just look for the silver triangles hanging from tree branches—they were all along the paths we took to the Apex and should make it easy to find the base."

Trail markers. Definitely missed those on the way up. Given that Abe and Gabby look up when Lemon relays this information, most of our classmates probably did too. They must've been what Mr. Tempest was referring to when he talked about the importance of attention to detail earlier.

"Now," Lemon continues, "Annika and Mystery will be

watching from above, so I'll create a distraction that'll keep them from seeing who's headed where."

"A distraction?" Abe asks. "As in a fire?"

"In a *forest*?" Gabby adds.

"Don't worry." Lemon answers them but looks at me. "It'll be completely contained."

They seem skeptical but keep typing.

"That should give us enough time to reach the base and get situated. Abe, can you do something that gets Mystery's attention right when they land?"

"Like tag the side of the golf cart?"

"Perfect. Gabby, would you mind standing guard and staring down any Troublemaker who comes down the main trail before our mission's complete?"

"It'd be my pleasure."

"Great. As you guys are doing that, we'll be hiding on the cart."

That's it? No special assignment for me? Could I be so lucky?

"Seamus," Lemon says, "while Mystery's distracted by Abe, you'll deliver the final blow."

Guess not.

I don't panic, though. At least, not right away. Lemon's plan is ambitious—and complicated. I wouldn't say so out loud, but I doubt we'll be able to pull it off. I'm so doubtful, in fact, I play my role as best I can. I hurry down trails (making sure to avoid Elinor's, since I don't want to lie to her) and share the fake challenge with such excitement Troublemakers barely hear the whole thing before sprinting toward the Apex. I find the silver triangles easily and follow them to the base. When the smell of smoke fills the air, I turn, note the individual gray plumes reaching for the sky, and keep walking. At the bottom of the mountain, I climb into the stretch golf cart, which Abe's already working on, and wait.

Lemon boards next. Through the window, I see Gabby hiding behind a pine tree near the head of the main trail. Lemon motions for me to duck behind a seat, which I do.

And *then* I panic. What will I throw? How? Should I miss, the way I meant to with Fern in the Kommissary? But can I intentionally foil the plan when the other alliance members did their parts? Won't they hate me? Will I survive the rest of the semester with no friends and more enemies than I've ever had?

Despite the cold, I'm suddenly hot. I'm breathing so fast my lungs strain to keep up. I think I might pass out, or worse, have a heart attack. Maybe I'll die right here, right now. That would be some mark to leave on Kilter's illustrious legacy . . . but at least it would get me out of doing what I'm supposed to do.

"You've got to be kidding me."

I hold my breath. That was Lemon. And he didn't bother whispering.

I come out of my crouch and peer over the seat back. He's sitting a few rows up, looking down and shaking his head. I move slowly, carefully toward him, like the golf cart's wired and could blow any second.

"He did it. *How* did he do it?"

"Who?" I ask, coming up behind them. "What?"

Lemon raises his K-Pak so I can see the screen. A video plays. It takes me a second to figure out what I'm watching, but then I see Troublemakers. The carousel. Three gold rings.

And a gleaming silver scooter . . . with attached sidecar.

"Mystery. He got us."

Chapter 16

DEMERITS: 1060
GOLD STARS: 180

It's too bad the Kommissary doesn't sell faculty-tracking devices. According to the Krew's last e-mail, trying to get Mystery earned me three hundred demerits. Subtracting all the gold stars I've gotten for calling the Hoodlum Hotline, and the cost of my only purchase, I now have eight hundred and sixty credits. And I'd spend every single one of those on something that might help us understand exactly what happened on that mountain.

We still don't get how Mr. Tempest did it. How did he know

what Lemon's fake note said, or that the other Troublemakers were at the top of the mountain while we waited at the base? Even more puzzling, how was he able to get a Kilter Series 9000 scooter with attached sidecar, neither of which we knew existed and both of which went to Jillian, whose long legs helped her beat our classmates up and down the mountain—delivered to Annika's Apex in minutes? Does he have an entire secret army of Troublemakers following us as they spy for him? Does Annika? Even so, wouldn't we have seen them? Or if they were that well hidden, wouldn't they have been smoked out by Lemon's stone-pit fires? With all those questions, we've come up with only one answer, and that's that Mystery's nickname suits him.

I'm still trying to figure it out a week later when Lemon throws open the door and bursts into our room.

"Happy Thanksgiving!"

In bed, I close the comic book I've been pretending to read and sit up. "It's Thanksgiving?"

"Yup." He crosses the room and opens our closet.

I grab my K-Pak from my desk and open the calendar. I've been too busy to keep track of days, but Lemon's right. I love stuffing, which Mom only makes on Thanksgiving, so I learned long ago that the holiday always falls on the fourth Thursday in November. And that's what today is.

"We have an hour before dinner," Lemon says. "Not much time, but enough."

He hands me my fleece. Puts my sneakers by my feet.

"Enough time for what?" I ask.

He stands up straight, slides his hands into his parka pockets . . . and smiles. And not just sort of smiles, with one corner of his mouth kind of higher than the other. For the first time, *both* corners of Lemon's mouth lift at the same time. I didn't know it was physically possible.

This is so nice to see that I put on my jacket and sneakers. I follow him without questioning where we're going or why. His smile grows as we walk, so I hardly notice when we duck behind a bush just outside the main classroom building as two Good Samaritans pass. Or when he uses a silver key card only faculty and staff members carry to unlock the entrance. Or when he leads me down a dark, narrow stairwell I've never climbed before, through a bright, wide tunnel that reminds me of a hospital corridor, and to an unmarked steel door.

It's only when he takes a deep breath and says, "Let's hope

this works," that the fish sticks I ate at lunch begin to swim in my belly.

"Lemon," I whisper, glancing down the hallway. "Where are we? What are we—"

He holds up one hand. Nods to a flashing silver pad to the right of the door. Takes off his backpack and carefully pulls out a small plastic bag. Inside the bag is a sparkly silver glove.

"That's Annika's." I know this because you can't miss her when she wears them; sunlight glints off the sequins and blinds all who pass. "Where did you—? How did you—?"

"Swiped it from her breakfast tray this morning. It was almost too easy. You'd think the director of a school for Troublemakers would be more cautious."

He pulls at the top of the bag, and the plastic snaps open. Then, careful not to touch the material directly, he turns both the glove and bag inside out. When he's done, the glove lies on the flattened plastic, palm side up. He holds this in one raised hand, like it's a plate of spaghetti and he's a waiter, and uses his other hand to slide the silver key card through the slot above the flashing pad.

HELLO, ANNIKA KILTER

The digital letters flash before me.

"You took her card, too?" I ask.

"That was trickier. I had to hide under the faculty table and snoop through her purse."

I'm impressed and stunned at the same time. Stealing things from our teachers is one thing—and encouraged. But from Annika? Isn't that going too far?

PLEASE PROCEED WITH PRINT IDENTIFICATION

Lemon tilts his hand so the glove stands at an almost ninety-degree angle. As he nears the pad, I hold my breath and check both ends of the hallway again.

"Done," Lemon says as the print pad beeps. "We're in."

The steel door whirrs, then slides into the wall.

"In where?" I ask.

It looks like some sort of control room. There are work-stations with computers. Radio receivers. A bunch of other electronic equipment I don't recognize. As we step inside, I see that large television screens fill three walls. A digital map of the United States, labeled TROUBLEMAKER TERRITORIES and covered in silver and black dots, takes up the fourth. A long, clear confer-ence table lined with clear, high-backed chairs sits in the middle of the room. A silver laptop is placed before each chair, and a glittery "KA" statue stands tall on the center of the table.

"I don't know," Lemon says. "Not exactly, anyway."

"Then what are we doing here?"

He steps farther into the room, faces me.

"When I was in the Kommissary the other day," he says, "I overhead Wyatt and Samara talking. Wyatt said he was so excited to speak to his brother that afternoon because it was his brother's birthday. Samara was excited for him and said that while K-Mail's great and superefficient, nothing compares to real, live conversation."

He pauses.

"And?" I say.

"And . . ." The corners of his mouth lift higher as his feet shuffle backward. "Voilà."

He pushes the "KA" statue aside. Behind it is another piece of electronic equipment.

Only this one I recognize.

"Is that . . . ?" I take one step. Another. "That looks like a . . ."

"A phone? A *real* phone, with twelve buttons that can dial real numbers?" Lemon nods. "Yup."

I look at him. "How did you find this?"

"I trailed Wyatt. All day. At first I didn't know if teachers were allowed personal cell phones, and if that were the case, I would've waited for Wyatt to call his brother before swiping his. But he didn't use a cell phone. He came here late at night, when no one else was around. I snuck in after him and trailed him to right outside this room. The door slid shut before I could slip in, but I heard him talking and laughing. It wasn't a long conversation, but it was definitely a conversation."

My eyes shift from him to the phone and back to him as I process this. "And you brought me here because . . . ?"

"Because twelve Troublemakers gave up on me." He looks down, then up again. "But you didn't."

If we weren't guys, I'd totally hug him right now. Since we are, I settle for smiling back.

"Plus," he adds, "our closet isn't exactly Fort Knox."

"What do you mean?"

"I mean, unless you like talking back to imaginary people, you don't really go in there to watch bad movies."

My cheeks warm. I open my mouth to offer some other explanation, but none comes out.

"It's no big deal," Lemon says quickly. "But you miss your parents, right? And you keep trying Marla because you think she'll crack and call them for you?"

"Maybe," I mumble.

"So then here you go." He pats the phone. "A small Thanksgiving gift from me to you. Because I'm thankful you're my roommate."

I don't know what to say. I'm embarrassed he knows about my calling the Hoodlum Hotline, even if he doesn't know the real reasons why, but I'm more touched that he went to all this trouble to do something nice for me. So while part of me is tempted to refuse the gift—and his assumption—a bigger part still wants to hug him.

Because it's a *phone.* All I have to do is press eleven numbers, and I'll hear my parents' voices for the first time in six weeks.

So, "Thanks," I say.

"You're welcome." He checks his watch. Claps his hands once. "Gotta run."

"What?" I turn as he hurries past me. "Where?"

"Annika probably knows her stuff's missing by now. I'm sure she'll be looking for it, so I'm creating a diversion."

"How?"

He stops by the door, takes a lighter from his parka pocket, and flicks it open, releasing an orange flame. "The usual ways." He snaps the lighter closed. "Don't worry, I'll come get you. But if you smell smoke, run."

He leaves. The door slides shut behind him. It's just me, a bunch of beeping, flashing electronic equipment . . . and my parents.

The reality of this hits me. I bolt toward the table, yank out a chair. Drop into the seat and pull the phone closer. I take the receiver in one hand, noting that it feels strange and familiar at the same time.

And then I think about what I'll say.

Hi, Mom! It's Seamus!

Mother, it's me! Your son!

Mama! Long time, no speak. What's shaking?

Hola, mi madre! *How's the stuffing?*

Hi, Mom. How are you? Happy Thanksgiving!

That's it. Polite yet warm. I don't bother brainstorming what to say after that, because Mom will probably start crying right away. I hope she misses me, but even if she's still too upset about what I did for that, she must be missing Thanksgivings past, when life was normal. Hearing my voice will remind her of those happier days and bring on the waterworks, which will give me plenty of time to figure out what to say next.

I bring the receiver to my ear. Take a deep breath. And dial.

The phone rings. Once. Twice. It's halfway through the third ring when someone picks up—and loud music slams into my head like a Mack truck. The force drives the phone from my ear.

"Happy Thanksgiving!" Mom's singing when I bring the receiver back.

My heart lifts. I start to say the same thing but stop. The music—rock, no less—is strange, but that's not the only thing that doesn't sound quite right.

"Helloooo?"

There are voices in the background. I barely make out Dad's, which is muffled by several others. They're loud too. Happy.

"Is anyone there?"

I press the receiver hard against my ear. Listen closely. Someone laughs—only the sound is more like a groan broken up by snorts.

I know that laugh.

"Oh well!" Mom's voice softens as she starts to put down the phone. "Must be a wrong number!"

It belongs to Bartholomew John.

Chapter 17

DEMERITS: 1060
GOLD STARS: 180

I don't know how long I sit there with the receiver pressed to my ear. At some point, the dial tone starts beeping. At another, the door whooshes open and Lemon bursts into the room. This snaps me out of my hypnosis, and I hang up.

"How was it?" he asks, breathless.

"Great." I force a smile. "Couldn't have been better."

"Awesome." He leans back through the open doorway and looks down the hall. "Ready to make like a turkey and fly?"

"Turkeys fly?" I say.

His head turns toward me. His furry eyebrows lift.

"Right." I stand up, push in the chair. "Not important."

I follow him out of the room. We take a different route from the one we took earlier and leave from an emergency exit on the side of the building. The air's chilly and smells like smoke.

"Dumpster," Lemon says, seeing me look around. "Self-contained but big enough to occupy all on-duty Good Samaritans."

"Nice."

We walk away from the building quickly—but not *too* quickly. We don't want to invite attention by fleeing the scene of the crime. At first I worry Lemon will ask more questions about my phone call, but he doesn't. Not even when we're far enough away from the fire that I no longer smell it, and his shoulders slump forward as he relaxes.

This gives me time to process what just happened. Or try to, anyway. If I had weeks instead of minutes, I still wouldn't figure it out.

Because what *was* that? Our Thanksgivings are always nice and quiet. Dad cleans, Mom cooks, and I set the table. We sit down, talk about how grateful we are for good health and family, and eat. Sometimes Dad puts on one of his old, mellow hippie records, but most times there's no music; the *pop* the sparkling cider bottle makes as it's opened is as rowdy as it gets. And never, not once in my twelve years on earth, have we ever had company.

Do they hate me that much that they invited my arch-nemesis over for a rip-roaring party? To show me, in case I happened to call or stop by, how angry they are? That they're so upset they've already forgotten me and moved on?

And if that's the case, how could they sound so happy about it?

"Don't sweat it," Lemon says.

Which makes me realize my eyes are watering. He must have noticed and now thinks talking to my parents made me miss them even more than I did before. Not wanting him to worry—or regret giving me such a thoughtful gift—I blink back the tears. When new ones form, I press my sleeve to my eyes and leave it there a second, letting the fleece absorb the moisture.

My vision clearer, I see that while I was stressing, we walked all the way to the Kanteen. The dining hall's been transformed since lunch and is decorated with balloons, streamers, and fresh flowers. The bright overhead lights are dimmed, and tall, lit candles have been placed on every table, creating a warm glow throughout the room. Before each place setting is a pile of gifts wrapped in shiny silver paper.

"I guess this comes with being valedictorian." Lemon stands before the tallest stack in the first-year dining section. "You're more than welcome to all nonflammable items."

"Thanks," Abe says, joining us. "I'll be sure to take you up on that."

"Me too," Gabby says, coming up behind Abe. They both grin.

"Actually, no one will be taking Lemon up on that."

I stand up straighter as Annika approaches. So do my alliance-mates.

"It's okay," Lemon says. "There are so many, I don't mind sharing."

Annika stops. Smiles. She must be wearing special makeup tonight, because her face glitters in the candlelight.

"It's a generous offer . . . but your gifts are here." She places her hand on the chair to the left of the one Lemon claimed. That stack's nothing to sneeze at, but it's definitely a few inches shorter than the other.

"But I just checked my rank this morning," Lemon says. "I'm still first in the class."

"Indeed you are. And we're very proud of all you've accomplished. But *these* gifts"—Annika's hand lifts and floats to the chair Lemon still stands behind—"are for Seamus."

"Hinkle?" Abe says.

"Why?" Gabby asks. Then, "No offense, Seamus."

"It's okay," I say, heart racing. "It's probably just because I started late. And Annika and our teachers are so nice they wanted to really go out of their way to make me feel at home today. Right?"

I look at Annika. Her eyelashes are so sparkly, I almost miss them lowering and lifting as she winks.

"Right. And also because we got an unbelievable deal on some supercool, limited-edition movie memorabilia." She opens her arms. "Today, on Thanksgiving, we want each and every one of you to know how grateful we are that you're here. These gifts are just small tokens of our great appreciation for your hard work and cooperation. We hope you enjoy them."

And then, one by one, she gives us hugs. She holds on to me a split second longer than everyone else, but it's such a small difference I don't think anyone will notice. Plus, I'm not sure if she extends the embrace . . . or if I do. Because hugging Annika makes me think of Mom hugging me before bed each night. And that makes me not want to let go.

But I do. And Annika moves down the table and on to the next group of Troublemakers. Abe discovers small silver name cards by our water glasses, and he and Gabby go off in search of theirs. Lemon and I sit, and I quickly turn my tall stack into two shorter stacks.

"Brr," Lemon says. "Ice queen's getting the cold shoulder."

I lean forward and peer between him and his gifts. At the very end of the table, Elinor sits with Marcus, who's talking with Annika. As I watch, Annika gives him the same smile and hug she gave everyone else, and then walks past Elinor without so much as a glance.

"Where are her presents?" I ask. All that's on the table before Elinor is a plate and silverware.

"Who knows?" Gabby says.

"Who cares?" Abe says. After circling the entire table, they return and find their seats to the right of mine.

I care. It's Thanksgiving. No one should feel excluded—especially not here, so far from friends and family.

"The Ventriloquist Vampire Collector's Set!" Abe declares,

holding up a box of graphic novels. "Awesome!"

He's already plowing through his gifts. So is Gabby. Lemon's not exactly tearing through wrapping paper, but he does hold one box to his ear and give it a small shake.

Personally, the last thing I want to do is open presents, even if they're supercool, limited-edition *Lord of the Rings* memorabilia, which, given the ring I now notice tied to a ribbon, is a good possibility. It doesn't feel right. I don't deserve them. On top of which, Thanksgiving at Kilter is like Christmas anywhere else, and thinking of Christmas makes me think of our quiet, festive mornings back home. What—or who—will I hear in the background if I call again December 25? Santa Claus himself? For three years I've doubted Santa showing up, but a visit from him was always a million times more likely than one from Bartholomew John.

At least, it was until today.

"Hey." Wearing a new Kilter baseball cap, Abe leans toward me and motions for Lemon to come closer. "Check it out. Think we should bring down the big guy tonight? Maybe spike his apple cider and then get him while his senses are dulled?"

We follow his nod to Mr. Tempest, who sits alone at the

faculty dining table while his coworkers mingle with older Troublemakers.

"No," Lemon says. "It's a holiday. Let him have the night off."

Abe pouts but doesn't protest. "Then can we at least come up with a name?"

"A name?" Lemon repeats.

Abe looks around, then leans so far over I can smell the root beer on his breath. "For the ance-illay," he whispers. "The lance-ilnay. The—"

"The alliance?" Lemon says.

Abe's chin drops just as Gabby wedges herself between him and the table.

"Hey." She bites into a chocolate turkey that's as big as her head. "I know I'm a girl, but I'm just as much a part of this allian—"

Abe's hand flies over her mouth. Her eyes widen, then almost immediately narrow and lock on his. No match for her expert stare, he removes his hand.

"Sorry," he says. "But can we please be a little less obvious? I'd like to use our advantage before we lose it."

"So you'd like to name our . . . salad fork?" Lemon takes the utensil from the table and holds it up.

Abe starts to shake his head. Lemon tilts his.

"Oh! *Yes.*" Abe tries to appear casual as he glances across the table and over both shoulders. "Yes, I'd *love* to name our salad fork. Because it's a *Kilter* salad fork and is *so* very *different* from *ordinary* salad forks."

Gabby takes another bite, decapitating the turkey. "Slick, A-Man."

"Ooh." Abe turns back. Lowers his voice. "How about A-Team? Too much?"

They start discussing possibilities. I start to tune out—just as something hits the back of my head. I look down and see a small rubber pilgrim next to my sneaker. When I pick it up, the pressure from my fingers make its eyes balloon like it was just attacked by an enemy's arrow. I turn it over and find a folded piece of paper taped to its back.

Seamus,

If you're not careful, you'll freeze to death in the New World.

Thanks for making my job easy. Fun, too.

Ike

P.S. It's a good thing the Brits didn't go DOWN UNDER for their religious freedom. If they had, who knows where we'd be?

I look behind me and scan the crowd. Not surprisingly, my tutor's nowhere in sight. I reread the note, then peer under the tablecloth. Finding nothing but discarded ribbons and wrapping, I check under my chair.

And there it is. A lumpy, brown grocery bag. There's nothing shiny or fancy about the packaging; as I pull it out, I see dark splatters near the bottom, like it once held fried chicken. And maybe it *still* holds fried chicken. I don't really deserve that, either, but judging by other kids' gifts, it's definitely more appropriate than whatever's in my stacks of unopened boxes.

Only it's not fried chicken. It's not fried anything. It's a brand-new, tags-on, down winter parka.

Black. Just like Ike's.

"Nice."

I look up to find Lemon looking at me. He sits back in his chair, apparently waiting for Abe and Gabby to stop arguing over whether "Abraham's Army" works as an alliance name.

"Weird that it's not silver," he adds, "but nice."

"Thanks," I say. "I'm going to try it out."

He nods. I stand up. Gabby drops into my empty seat without asking why I'm leaving.

I try to smile as I hurry through the main dining room. I still can't see Ike, but that doesn't mean he can't see me, and I want him to know I appreciate the gift. I even go outside so it seems like I'm doing what I told Lemon I would. By the entrance, I step to the left of the glass doors and count to thirty. To be on the safe side, I re-enter the building at the back of a pack of Trouble-makers.

And then I bolt for the nearest restroom.

There's a kid washing his hands when I burst through the door. Not wanting to invite suspicion—or even curiosity—I give him a casual wave before slipping into a stall. As I wait for him to finish, I think about what I'll tell Ike when I'm not wearing the parka at our next training session. I lost it? Someone stole it? Lemon accidentally set it on fire?

The running water stops. The door opens and closes. I unlock and step out of the stall—and immediately step back in when I see Devin, my music teacher and only remaining faculty target besides Mr. Tempest. He must've come in as the other Troublemaker was leaving.

I hold my breath and peer through the narrow space between the stall door and frame. Devin would have to walk past me to get to the urinals . . . but he doesn't. He stays by the sinks. Takes a small white box from the pocket of his jeans. And starts flossing.

I think this can't last long, but it does. He spends more time on one tooth than I do on my entire mouth—and Mom's big on dental hygiene, so I'm no slouch. I'd leave and do what I came to do later, but I haven't made a sound since he entered the room. He doesn't know I'm here. If I go now, he might wonder what I've been doing, why I've been so quiet. At the very least, my sudden, unexpected presence will definitely freak him out. So much so I might even be able to cross him off my list.

I think about this. Do I *want* to cross him off? I got every other teacher accidentally, but this would be intentional. If I succeeded, I'd be a real Troublemaker—not just a kid who stumbles into trouble more often than most regular kids. How could I go home after that? Knowing I intentionally did something my parents wouldn't approve of, after everything else I've done?

But then I remember how happy Mom sounded on the

phone. And how happy Lemon looked when he presented me with the phone.

And I pucker my lips and whistle.

It's high-pitched. Short. Out in the crowded dining room the sound would be lost, but in here it bounces and reverberates off tiles and porcelain. And it has the desired effect.

Devin drops the box of floss. Grabs his chest with one hand. Spins around.

"Who's there?" he demands.

I bite back a smile. Whistle again. Louder this time, so he thinks I'm closer than I am.

He lunges for the first stall and pushes open the door. When it's empty, he tries the next one, and the one after that. I move too, placing the black parka on the floor so it muffles my knees and sneakers as I shimmy under stall dividers. I whistle every few seconds, which makes him stop and try to gauge where the noise is coming from.

But he can't figure it out. And eventually, he throws up his hands, grabs the floss from the floor, and leaves.

"Congratulations," he shoots over his shoulder before the door closes behind him.

I wait a few seconds, then step out of the stall. I go to the trash can and ball up the coat. My automatic instinct when I opened Ike's gift was to get rid of it. His black parka stands out from the silver parkas and is a glaring reminder that he's different from other Troublemakers. Since coming to Kilter I've worked hard to blend in, to not be any more different than I already was.

But something changed today. *I* changed today.

So I don't throw away the coat. I shake it out. Brush it off.

And put it on.

Chapter 18

DEMERITS: 1260
GOLD STARS: 180

Plastic or stainless steel?"

I check out the two discs Ike holds up. One looks like a regular Frisbee, the other like something a lumberjack might use to buzz down a small tree.

"Stainless steel," I say.

"Really?" His smile dips. "I was kind of kidding. We always start you on the beginner model."

"What can I say? I'm feeling adventurous today."

"All righty then." He moves to hand me the silver disc, then seems to think better of it and pulls back. "Everything's okay, right? No trouble in paradise?"

"Paradise?"

"With Ice Queen Elinor?"

The closest Elinor and I have come to paradise is a late-night sprint across campus that ended with me face-first in the river. Before I can explain that there's no trouble for this very reason, Ike continues.

"The Boomaree, so named for being part boomerang, part Frisbee, is a powerful weapon. Heightened emotions can lead to reckless—and potentially dangerous—use."

"Everything's fine," I say. "I'm just in the mood to have fun and bank some demerits."

This seems to satisfy him. He nods and hands me the silver disc. I take it and peer out from behind the storage shed. Fifty feet away, members of the Sniper Squad swing bats at seemingly indestructible mailboxes.

"Am I aiming for the kids or the mailboxes?" I ask.

"Neither. This type of aerial assault is infinitely more effective without physical contact." Ike waits for me to look at him, then nods toward a bench across the lawn and away from the squad. "Allow me to demonstrate."

I jog to the bench. I haven't even turned around when there's a sharp buzz by my right ear. I swat at the noise reflexively, thinking mosquitoes must've adapted to the cold this far north . . . but then I hear it again. By my left ear this time. I swat. Spin. Search the air for winged insects. Swat and spin some more when the buzz sounds so close to my right ear I worry the bug's flown inside. When the buzz moves to my left ear, I tilt my head to the side and hop, like the source will fall out the way water does after an underwater swim.

I'm still hopping when Ike taps me on the shoulder. I stop and realize the buzzing has too.

"What's so funny?" I ask.

It takes a second for Ike to stop chuckling. "Ants in your pants?"

"Actually, I think they were—" My eyes fall to the Frisbee he taps against his leg. "Wow. How'd you do that?"

"It's all in the wrist. Well, that and this handy sensor." He holds up a small black box with a red button. "There's one on the bottom of your disc. Remove the box before you throw, hit the button when you're ready, and the disc will loop right back to you. Good for the environment—and creating maximum confusion."

I turn over the silver disc. The box is so small I wouldn't have seen it if Ike hadn't pointed it out. "So the goal is to mess with the target rather than hit it?"

"Exactly. Though if you *do* make contact, it's not the worst thing in the world. You won't drive someone crazy when he can clearly see what hit him—but you'll still annoy him." Ike jogs backward. "The steel's even faster. I'd recommend a few practice shots to get the hang of it."

I take the shots. The first few are way off; some fly several feet over and past Ike's head, others crash to the ground between us. Bringing the disc back is also harder than it looks. The timing has to be exactly right—ideally, when the target's spinning in confusion—or the disc will be seen and your cover blown.

But I'm focused. Just like I've been since Thanksgiving. And after a dozen or so tries, Ike thinks I'm ready to try out my newest weapon on the mailbox maulers.

"Ten demerits per rotation," he whispers once we're looking out from behind the storage shed again.

The closest Troublemaker is a kid named Greg Pearlman. He's tall, skinny, and clumsy with a bat. That might be because it weighs about as much as he does. I wait for his eyes to lock on the mailbox as he pulls the bat behind him before flicking the Boomaree.

It zips just over his right shoulder. He does a half spin. Holding the box in my fist, I squeeze once. The disc zips back, nearly grazing his left shoulder and propelling him into another half spin. As he stumbles and looks around, I open my other hand. The disc's cool edge smacks into my palm.

"Ten," Ike whispers.

"Nice," a familiar female voice whispers.

I spin around. Annika leans out of her golf cart, toward me.

"Thank you," I say.

"Thank *you*," Annika says with a wink. Then she brings two fingers to her forehead, gives Ike a mini salute, and keeps driving. She stops again near the mailbox maulers to offer a few tips on form and speed before continuing on and disappearing over a small hill.

"Ready?" Ike asks.

Bolstered by Annika's praise, I eye the row of Troublemakers for a more challenging target, finally settling on Elias Montero. He's the same height as Greg but wider, more muscular. Probably because when we're all lying on couches in the TV lounge, he's doing push-ups and sit-ups in the corner of the room. He doesn't look like the kind of guy who'd freak out over a few strange noises.

But looks can be deceiving. Because ten seconds later, after the Boomaree's made a triple loop and is back in my hand, he's still spinning.

"Thirty," Ike whispers. Grins. "Imagine how freaked out your parents will be when you try this at home."

He says this just as I'm releasing the Boomaree on my third target. I lose focus for a split second—and the silver disc zooms over the line of Troublemakers and disappears on the other side of the hill.

"That's okay," Ike says. "Just bring it back and try again."

I tighten my fist. Watch the top of the hill. When the disc doesn't appear, I squeeze harder, longer. That doesn't work, so I switch hands, place the box on my open palm, and hold down the red button with one finger.

Nothing.

"Could it be out of range?" I ask.

Ike shakes his head. "Not that fast. It must've hit something."

I feel bad instantly. He was nice enough to let me start with the stainless steel Boomaree, and now I've lost it. Maybe even broken it. Not wanting to disappoint him further, I pocket the sensor and start jogging.

"Be right back!" I call over my shoulder.

I run across the field, dodging flailing limbs and swinging bats as I cut through the line of Troublemakers. As I run I wonder how much a Boomaree goes for in the Kommissary. I earned a hundred demerits for getting Devin and some more for completing class assignments, bringing my last total to twelve hundred and sixty. And I've stopped calling the Hoodlum Hotline, so my gold star tally is holding steady at a hundred and eighty. After subtracting the only twenty I've spent (on the Kilter Pocket Extinguisher), I have one thousand and sixty credits left. That has to be enough to buy at least one stainless steel Boomaree.

At the top of the hill I pause and scan the garden on the other side. I'm about to run down for a closer look when I hear a familiar voice.

"Who does she think she is? *Where* does she think she is? And when did it become okay to show absolutely zero respect to the people who are trying to help you? The ones who take you in when no one else wants you?"

Annika. She barks into a walkie-talkie as she storms down the steps of a nearby gazebo and climbs into her golf cart. It takes off with a jerk in the opposite direction.

Thinking the display strange but none of my business, I start down the hill. As I do, the wind shifts, and I stop again to listen.

Tree branches creak. In the distance, kids talk and laugh. Deciding I must be imagining things, I take another step.

But there it is again—a soft, light noise that sounds a little like someone singing. Only the noise wavers. It's interrupted by sniffles and nose blowing.

And it seems to come from the direction Annika just left.

Forgetting about the Boomaree, I continue down the hill, slower now, and head for the gazebo. My chest tightens when I glimpse a long, red braid through the structure's wooden slats. It's still none of my business . . . but my feet move faster anyway. Before my brain can talk my body out of it, I'm charging up the steps and standing in the doorway.

"Are you okay?"

Elinor gasps. Looks up. Scrambles to gather the photos that surround her. There are dozens of them; some are in color, many are in black and white. Tears fall from her eyes, blurring some of the images before I can make out what they are. She takes them by the handful and shoves them between the pages of an open book. When she's done, she closes the book, puts both hands on the cover, and presses down—like if she can only apply enough pressure, the photos will disintegrate and she'll never have to see them again.

Eventually, she removes her hands. The book cover springs up. She sits back, unties the green satin ribbon from her braid, and uses it to wipe her eyes. I wait for her to demand to know what I'm doing there, to yell at me to go away and leave her alone, but she doesn't.

To be honest, part of me wishes she would. Then I wouldn't have to stand there awkwardly, wanting to help but having no idea how.

"If you're looking for Mr. Tempest," she finally says, her voice even, "you won't find him here."

I pause. "Mr. Tempest?"

She looks up. "Isn't that what you and your friends have been doing all week? Following him around to figure out when and where you might surprise him?"

Three responses come to mind immediately. The first is that with the exception of Lemon, the alliance members aren't my friends. The second is that we're not as sneaky as we think we are if Elinor knows what we've been up to. The third is the one I go with.

"I wasn't looking for him." I step into the gazebo. "I was looking for you."

I'm aware as I say the words that they sound like ones some cheesy guy would say in some cheesy romance movie. But I'm also aware that they're true . . . and that Elinor's face softens slightly when she hears them.

Afraid she might bolt if I come any closer, I lower myself to the ground. As we sit quietly, I look around. Outside, the gazebo's rimmed in tall bushes; their branches are bare now, but there are enough of them that the gazebo still feels enclosed, protected inside. Small white lights are strung from the roof, making the space glow against the gray dusk. It's quiet. Cozy. The kind of place a cheesy guy would love to be with a pretty girl.

"She's mad at me," Elinor says, bringing me back to the reason we're here.

"Who?"

"Annika. She thinks I'm not doing enough. That I don't want to be here."

"*Do* you want to be here?"

She shrugs. "There are worse places."

I'm curious to know what qualifies as worse but guess there are better times to ask.

"She said I need to work harder or face the consequences."

"Like what?" I ask. "Being kicked out?"

Elinor nods. I think about some of the other times I've seen her since coming to Kilter. Sitting across from me that first night at dinner. Staring out the window in math class. Reading on the bench in the garden. Standing in the doorway of the Performance Pavilion viewing box. Lagging behind on the hike to Annika's Apex. Sitting, without presents, in the Kanteen at Thanksgiving. Always quiet. Usually alone.

"Do you *want* to go home?" I ask.

She brings the book to her chest, rests her chin on its top. "I want a home to go back to."

At least, that's what I think she says. The words are so soft, so fast, the breeze sweeps them away the instant they're spoken.

"Maybe I can talk to Annika," I say.

She looks at me. "About what?"

"About, I don't know . . . your situation. Maybe I can ask her to go easy on you, to cut you some slack."

Her copper eyes, which were so warm a second ago, cool. "And what makes you think she'd care about what one first-year student says about another first-year student?"

Because I'm Kilter's first murderer. A natural-born Troublemaker. And now that I'm actually embracing my training, I'm probably meeting Annika's high expectations.

"Never mind." Elinor jumps up. Hugs the book. Hurries across the gazebo. "It doesn't matter."

"Wait." I jump up too. "Please don't go. I'm sorry. It's none of my business. I just wanted to help."

She stops in the doorway. For a second I think she'll turn around and thank me for my concern. But she doesn't. She stands with her back to me and says, "He runs."

Again, I'm stumped. "Who?"

"Mr. Tempest. At midnight, when everyone else is asleep. He does a three-mile loop through the main garden, starting and ending at the Kanteen."

"How do you—"

Know? That's what I'd ask if Elinor hung around long enough to hear the question. Instead she leaves.

And I'm alone in the gazebo.

I'm tempted to go after her, but I know she doesn't want to be followed. To give her space before I return to Ike, who might be gone by now, I sit back down and take my K-Pak from my backpack. I'm about to check my K-Mail when the breeze parts the branches, letting in a sliver of sunlight. The light glints off a piece of paper I hadn't noticed near my foot, and I reach forward to pick it up.

It's not just a piece of paper—it's a picture. Of two young girls riding horses on a beach. One has long, dark hair and looks familiar; after squinting and examining closely, I decide this is Annika as a teenager. The other appears to be a few years younger. She has darker hair and also looks familiar, but I can't place her. Is she another Kilter staff member? A teacher?

When I finally figure out why she looks familiar, I'm glad the gazebo wall's there to fall back on.

It's her eyes. They're warm. Soft. Reddish brown.

Just like worn pennies.

Chapter 19

DEMERITS: 1390
GOLD STARS: 180

I'm not sure this is such a good idea," I say.

"I am," Abe says.

"But it's so complicated. Dangerous, even."

"Only if something goes wrong," Gabby says. "Which it won't."

"How do you know?" I ask.

"We don't." Lemon hands me a walkie-talkie. "But we're as prepared as we can be."

I sit back on the bed and watch them get ready. It's been a

week since my run-in with Elinor, six days of which have been spent planning and strategizing for Mr. Tempest's takedown. I didn't tell the alliance about what happened in the gazebo, but I did mention to Lemon that I thought I overheard an older Troublemaker say at breakfast that our history teacher is a late-night track star. Lemon confirmed this hours later by ducking and hiding behind rocks, bushes, and trash cans as he trailed Mr. Tempest through the darkness. An emergency alliance meeting was called the next morning, and we've been plotting ever since.

Or *they've* been plotting. I've been listening. And thinking about Elinor. Who hasn't spoken to me since fleeing the gazebo.

"Would it help if we went over the plan of attack one more time?" Lemon asks.

Probably not, but I nod anyway. Maybe hearing it again will convince one of them we're in over our heads.

"Okay. So." Lemon points his walkie-talkie antenna at the campus map taped to our closet doors. Mr. Tempest's route is marked in yellow highlighter and broken up by a series of silver star stickers. "There are three miles and four of us. Gabby's up first, at the one-mile mark. As soon as she hears Mystery coming closer, she'll jump out and hypnotize him with her weird alien eyes."

At this, the overhead light goes out. A pair of glowing green eyes appear. They rise and fall, bobbing silently throughout the room as Gabby moves.

"Totally creepy," Abe says. "He's going to freak."

The lights come on. Gabby winks.

"Glow-in-the-dark contact lenses," she says. "Thank you, Kommissary."

"We hope he does freak, at least a little. That way he'll already be rattled by the time he reaches the second-mile marker." Lemon's radio antenna taps the next sticker on the map.

"Abe Henge," Abe says proudly. "Like Stonehenge but scarier. Here Mystery will lose his way in a maze of clay and wood sculptures."

"If and when he gets out," Lemon says, "but most likely when, because this is Mystery we're talking about, he'll have a half mile to recover before entering Firebomb Boulevard, a dizzying stretch of pyrotechnics guaranteed to send him running directly to the Kanteen patio . . . where Seamus will take advantage of his lowered defenses to do him in, once and for all."

"Awesome," Abe says.

"Brilliant," Gabby says.

"Good Samaritans," I say.

Lemon's eyebrows lift. "What about them?"

"What if they catch us? This is so serious we'd probably be docked an entire month of troublemaking privileges." I shoot Abe a look. "That's plenty of time for our classmates to knock us to the bottom of the rankings."

"It's Friday night," Lemon says as Abe frowns. "The ones who aren't sleeping will be singing it up at the weekly staff karaoke party—which Mystery never attends. According to my tutor, the GS love getting their groove on . . . so we should be fine."

"How do we know he'll stick to his regular route once things start going down?" I ask. "Couldn't he just veer off, or turn around?"

Lemon puts down the walkie-talkie, picks up a plastic box, and faces the closet doors. Twenty seconds later Mr. Tempest's running route is surrounded by two dozen red pushpins.

"I've planted small yet effective subterranean explosives that'll go off under one hundred sixty pounds of pressure. My guess is Mystery weighs in at one sixty-five, one-seventy. The second he steps on one, he'll get a dent in his sneaker—and a push in the right direction." Lemon faces us again. "Any other questions?"

"Yeah. Can we get this show on the road already?" Abe jumps up from my desk chair and claps me on the back. "Relax, dude. It's not like we're going to kill the guy."

In the mirror over Lemon's dresser, I see my face freeze.

"And just think of all the awesome stuff we can buy with all the credits we're about to earn." Gabby half walks, half bounces as she follows Abe out the door.

"You all right?" Lemon asks when they're gone.

I jump up. Put on my coat. "Yup."

"You seemed fine with the plan all week. Did something happen to make you worry now?"

"No." I choose my words carefully. "It's just trouble. Serious trouble. Like, with a capital *T*."

His eyes widen. I don't want him to think I'm unhappy with him for being the plan's main mastermind, so I open my mouth to try to explain.

"That's perfect," he says.

My lower lip hits my upper lip.

He takes a marker from the desk and writes "CAPITAL T" in big black letters across the top of the map. He surveys it a second, then turns and looks at me.

"What do you think?" he asks. "For an alliance name?"

I think an alliance name, which we'd never agreed on after shooting down dozens of suggestions, is currently the least of my concerns. But I also think he's right. As far as names go, Capital T would be hard to beat.

"It's good," I say. "Really good."

He grins. Makes a fist and holds it toward me. I make one too, and bump his with mine.

"Just remember." His expression turns somber again. "This is as serious as it gets. Mystery's the last obstacle. Once we're over him, the rest is cake."

This is surprisingly reassuring. So when Lemon takes his shoe box of fire-starting supplies from his desk, I take my ammo-packed duffel bag from the floor. And then we join Abe and Gabby outside.

It's eleven thirty. The sky is pitch-black, the campus silent. After Lemon quietly shares our new alliance name with the others, who cover their mouths with their hands to muffle their loud excitement, we walk together without speaking until we're on the other side of the creek's footbridge. Then we stop and stand, shoulder to shoulder, and look out over the darkened garden. I listen for last-minute instructions, some final words of wisdom . . . but they don't come.

"See you on the other side," Lemon says.

And we break.

I'm stationed on the Kanteen rooftop deck. As I head that way, I think about Lemon's concern—and my reason for suddenly hesitating. Part of it was probably because I wasn't convinced we'd actually get to this point, so I didn't consider all the potential consequences. But a bigger part was Elinor. Between my phone call home on Thanksgiving and finding Elinor crying in the gazebo, I made trouble without worrying about who it affected and how. But seeing her like that, so sad and alone, reminded me of Miss Parsippany. Because I imagine that's how my substitute teacher must've felt in the cafeteria that day, when she didn't know anyone and only wanted to do her job well—and put herself in harm's way because of it. And thinking of Miss Parsippany made me think of Mr. Tempest. He's no newbie teacher, but the way he keeps to himself, he might as well be. We're about to make his life very difficult, and for what? A few extra demerits? A Kommissary shopping spree?

Relax, dude. It's not like we're going to kill the guy.

I shake my head against Abe's voice. Reaching the Kanteen, I charge up the outdoor steps that lead to the roof. My boots boom like grenades in the silence of night; the noise is so startling I stop and look around, certain it's roused fellow Troublemakers from their beds. When the lawn remains empty, I continue—a bit more slowly, lighter on my feet. At the top of the stairs I make a sharp right and run, head lowered, to the far stone wall. There I unpack my duffel bag, carefully arranging the bow and arrows, Hydra-Bombs, and Boomaree (which Ike found and yanked from a tree trunk while I was with Elinor) on the deck. Then I sling the loaded Kilter Painter 1000 over one shoulder and assume my position.

"Orange to Capital T. Do you copy?"

I take the walkie-talkie from my coat pocket.

"Copy," I say.

"Ditto," Gabby says.

"Word," Abe says.

"So far, so good? All systems go?" After we confirm that they are, Lemon adds, "Great. Stay in touch."

Nothing happens for several minutes. I crouch behind the wall and watch the patio down below, blowing into my cupped hands every now and then to keep them warm. I practice swinging the rifle up and out. I check my watch, my heart racing more with each minute that passes.

And then, finally, at twelve o'clock on the dot, our target appears. He wears a black tracksuit, gleaming silver sneakers, and earmuffs.

"Mystery in sight," I whisper into the walkie-talkie.

"Awesome," Lemon whispers back.

Mr. Tempest stretches. Reaches from side to side. Twists left, then right. Bends backward, then forward. Jogs in place. All with his back to me, seemingly oblivious to what's about to happen. If I were another kind of Troublemaker, I could take him out right now. It'd be an easy shot, most likely over and done with one paintball. But in order for us all to get credit, each alliance member has to participate in the plan. Plus, I don't really want to be the only one responsible for whatever goes down. So I simply watch and wait.

"Mystery on the move," I whisper when our target runs from the patio and into the garden.

"Copy," Lemon says. "Gabby?"

"Bring it on." Her voice is thin with excitement.

I'm pretty sure I hold my breath for the next eight minutes.

Then the walkie-talkie crackles—and I'm pretty sure I jump out of my skin.

"Target approaching," Gabby whispers. "Launching attack in five . . . four . . . three . . . two . . . one!"

Which is an anticlimactic countdown. Because nothing happens—at least not that we can hear. The radio's quiet for what feels like an hour. I hold it in front of my face and stare, like it'll start transmitting live video feed.

Eventually, there's more crackling. This is followed by silence and another short burst of static.

"Gabby," Lemon says. "Are you there?"

Nothing. I hold the walkie-talkie to my ear. Shake it.

"I—"

My heart stops. That was her.

"I can't—"

More crackling. Static.

"Gabby," Lemon says, his voice serious. "What's going on?"

A long, excruciating stretch of silence.

"I'm here," she half whimpers, half gasps. "But something happened."

"What?" Lemon demands.

Another pause. Then a soft moan and, "I can't *see*!"

"What do you mean you—"

Lemon's cut off by Abe. "I've got him. About ten yards away. Don't worry, this Mystery will be solved in five . . . four . . . three—"

"No!" I practically shout when the radio goes dead again. I squeeze it so tightly my fingers turn white.

For better or worse, this silence doesn't last long.

"I'm okay!" Abe declares.

My lungs relax. The air I've been holding whooshes through my mouth.

"But I'm stuck!"

My lungs freeze again.

"What do you mean?" Lemon asks. "How?"

"I mean I'm pinned under rocks and branches. The guy somehow snuck up behind me and trapped me in my own maze! I don't think anything's broken—but I can't move."

"Okay." Lemon's voice wavers slightly. "Don't panic. I'm up next, and there's no way he's getting through unscathed. Abe, stay put until we come for you. You might've hurt something you don't feel yet. Gabby, can you find your way to the edge of the garden?"

"I think so," she sniffs. "My eyes don't sting as much anymore."

"Good. Wait for us there." Lemon pauses. "Seamus?"

It takes my thumb a second to press the radio button. I swallow the dry knot in my throat before speaking. "I'm here."

"Great." Another pause. When Lemon speaks again, he sounds even more serious. "Just be ready. This could all be over way faster than we thought."

Which isn't the same as saying we're all about to die, but right now, it sure sounds like it.

Heart hammering, I rest the radio on the wall, shove two Hydra-Bombs in my coat pockets for backup, and raise the Kilter Painter 1000. I scan the lawn and patio, searching for any sign of movement. Soon the wind shifts in my direction, bringing with it the distinct smell of smoke. The air fills with short, loud pops—the underground explosives going off.

I lift the rifle higher. Peer down its long, shiny barrel. Grip it tighter to keep it from shaking.

"It's okay," I whisper. "You're a marksman. A *trained* marksman. You can do this."

The smell of smoke grows stronger. This seems to be taking way too long, and I'm beginning to think Lemon shocked our target so much he couldn't go any farther . . . but then a black-clad figure darts from the woods.

I close one eye for better aim and press my pointer finger to the trigger. "Bingo."

"ABORT!"

My eyes snap open and shift to the radio still on the wall.

"Do you copy?" Lemon shouts. "Abort mission!"

"Why?" Abe yells. "What's going on?"

"Mystery set my supplies on fire! My extinguishers exploded! I'm going for help before it spreads!"

Something slams behind me. I jump—and drop my rifle. It hits the wall, then falls over the other side, clattering to the cold stone twenty feet below. I spin around to grab my other weapons . . . but they're gone. All of them. The bow and arrows. The Boomaree. The remaining Hydra-Bombs. Nothing's left but my empty duffel bag.

"Um, guys?" Gabby says through the radio. "I don't want to freak anyone out . . . but it's karaoke night, remember? What if the Good Samaritans aren't prepared to help?"

I snatch the radio and start running. "I'm coming for you both. I'll be there as fast as I can."

I fly down the stairs and across the patio. I'm just about to sprint across the lawn when I glimpse a flash of light from the corner of my eye. It's soft, dull . . . and comes from inside the Kanteen.

I don't know exactly what happens next. What I *do* know is that one minute I'm outside and about to run for Capital T . . . and then, all of a sudden, I'm inside the main dining room, staring at the back of Mr. Tempest's head.

He's sitting at the faculty table—in Annika's chair. His legs rest where her dinner plate would be. His ankles are crossed, and his silver sneakers gleam even brighter in the glow of a lit fireplace. In one hand he holds a clear glass goblet filled with ice water; in the other, a cigar. My weapons litter the floor by his chair. Every few seconds he puffs on the cigar and chuckles softly.

Without taking my eyes from his head, I slowly reach into my coat pockets. I'm so focused it takes a second to realize that my fingers come out cold and wet. The Hydra-Bombs must've popped while I was running.

There's no way I can reach my other weapons without him noticing. I don't want to waste time or risk being caught by leaving and looking for more. From where I stand by the trash can, this leaves only one option.

A single red apple.

It's on the floor behind the bin, apparently missed by whoever tossed it and by the cleaning crew. It's half eaten . . . but if used correctly, still effective.

I pick it up. Then, thinking only of Lemon, Elinor, Abe, Gabby, and me—and *not* Mom, Dad, or even Miss Parsippany—I bring back my right arm, concentrate on the silver *K* on Mr. Tempest's jacket, and bring my arm forward.

The apple hits the K's center. Mr. Tempest gasps and jerks forward. The glass goblet falls to the floor and shatters. The cigar drops to the other side and fizzles out in the spreading water.

Bull's-eye.

At first Mr. Tempest doesn't move. Neither do I.

Did I do it again? Only this time, because I meant to?

I take a step toward him just as his torso lifts. His back straightens slowly, one vertebra at a time. Without turning around, he takes in a long breath, releases it, and speaks.

"Congratulations, Mr. Hinkle," he says quietly, evenly. "I hope you're proud of yourself."

And for the first time in a long time, I am.

Chapter 20

DEMERITS: 1910
GOLD STARS: 180

A few days later, just before dinner, Lemon and I are working on drawings for art class when someone knocks on our door. I answer it—and almost swing the door shut when a Good Samaritan's standing there.

"We were just doing homework." I hold up my picture. It's a cat with daggerlike claws and razor-sharp teeth. Not my preferred subject, but Wyatt had asked us to draw something that'd freak out our parents if we hung it on the fridge at home.

The Good Samaritan leans forward to examine it. "Nice lines. Good shading."

I lower the picture. He stands upright.

"Come with me," he says to us. "Please."

"Is there a problem?" Lemon asks, coming up behind me.

"Not yet," the GS says. "But if I were you, I wouldn't keep Annika waiting."

I look at Lemon. He shrugs. We put on our shoes, grab our coats, and follow the GS outside to a waiting golf cart.

"Any idea what this is about?" Abe asks. He's already in the golf cart. So is Gabby.

"Nope," Lemon says. "But I guess we're about to find out."

We get in. There are still a few empty seats, and I think we'll be picking up other Troublemakers, but then the cart shoots forward. It flies through the courtyard, past the Kanteen and Kommissary, and into the woods. Ten minutes later it stops in front of a building I've never seen before.

"Is this another school?" Gabby asks.

It's a good guess. The building's three stories tall. It's made of stone and wood and surrounded by towering evergreen trees. The front door is arched and wide, like a castle drawbridge.

Whatever's on the other side must be important. Official.

Just like Annika.

"Hello, Troublemakers!" she sings as the door slowly opens. "Welcome to my home."

In the floor-to-ceiling mirror behind her, I see the chin of every Capital T member drop at the same time.

"You *live* here?" Gabby asks.

"Like, for real?" Abe asks.

"I do. For real." Annika smiles and steps aside. "Won't you come in?"

My feet aren't the only ones stuck to the ground. Nobody moves until the Good Samaritan nudges Lemon, who half steps, half stumbles forward. Once he regains his balance and heads inside, we manage to walk after him.

"Would you like something to drink?" Annika asks as she closes the door. A second later a man wearing a white suit and silver bow tie appears. He pushes a glass cart filled with water bottles, juice boxes, and cans of soda.

We make our selections, then follow Annika down a long hallway. As we pass open doorways, I peek into rooms. There's an office. A library. Some sort of conference room. The spaces are light and airy, which is surprising since from the outside, the house looks a hundred years old. Annika must've done some serious renovating before moving in.

The hallway ends at a large dining room overlooking a sprawling green lawn and turquoise lake. A long glass table in the center of the room looks like it can seat thirty, but is set for five. Behind each chair stands a white-suited, silver-bow-tied staff member. In the corner, an older woman plays a white piano.

"Where would you like them?"

I turn toward the unfamiliar voice and find yet another staff member. This one wears a camera around his neck.

"By the windows is fine," Annika says.

The photographer ushers us to the other side of the table. He takes a series of pictures, including individual shots as well as group ones. Annika tells us to stand tall and smile wide, which we do.

The session lasts several minutes. When it's over, the photographer leaves and the white-suited waiters pull out our chairs. As we sit, I glance at the rest of Capital T. Like me, they're smiling. Also like me, the corners of their mouths aren't fully lifted. We're happy to be here . . . but we're not sure *why* we're here.

Fortunately, Annika explains.

"I don't usually invite first-year Troublemakers to my home. That's a privilege reserved for fourth-year students who have proven themselves over eight semesters, and who are about to begin their post-Kilter troublemaking adventures." She motions to her waiter, who takes a glass bottle from a silver ice bucket. "I don't often extend early invitations—and never before a single semester has been completed." She pauses as the waiter pops the cork. "Do you know why I've made an exception today?"

"Because we got Mr. Tempest?" Abe guesses.

"Getting Mr. Tempest is why you got extra demerits. But you're on the right track."

"Because we got Mr. Tempest and no one got hurt?" Gabby tries. Considering that Lemon found and returned with the Good Samaritans in minutes, and that Abe wasn't hurt by the rock that fell on him, and that Gabby's eyes were totally fine after the Mace wore off, this is a good possibility.

"Still on the right track," Annika says. "But no."

I try to think of another reason but can't. My fellow alliance members seem to be having trouble too, because no one speaks.

"Seamus threw the apple," Annika finally says, which makes

my face burn so hot I drain my water glass—and the next two my waiter brings me. "Technically, it was his hit that took Mr. Tempest down. But you all received extra credit because you all worked together to get to that point. You were a team."

A team. Not an alliance. Is there a difference?

"As you know," Annika continues, "Kilter promotes individual goals and achievements. This leads to healthy competition that encourages students to work harder and really push themselves. It's not until much later, when students have grown on their own, that we try to foster collaborative troublemaking. Some never learn to work together. Others try but continue to put their personal interests before the group's."

I hold up the champagne flute by my plate as her waiter comes around. He fills the glass with sparkling apple cider.

"Your plan to get Mr. Tempest was complicated. Risky. It shouldn't have worked, and it almost didn't. Each of you could've bailed at any point . . . but you didn't. In not doing so, you displayed skill and maturity beyond your years and experience." Annika raises her glass of cider. "So I'd like to propose a toast."

Lemon and I exchange excited smiles and raise our glasses too. Across the table, Abe and Gabby do the same.

"To four of the best first-year Troublemakers Kilter's ever had. May your careers be long and successful."

The table's so big it takes some acrobatic maneuvering, but we all reach and stretch until every glass has been clinked together. Then we drink.

"In celebration, my chefs have prepared your favorite foods," Annika says as our waiters bring out silver platters. "Your photos will be displayed in the Performance Pavilion, on the Kilter Academy Wall of Fame. And most importantly, you now have the opportunity to do something first-years—and second- and third-years—normally only dream of doing."

"Going on an all-expenses-paid Kommissary shopping spree?" Abe asks.

His question makes me think of the five hundred demerits I got for defeating Mystery. I have so many credits now, there's not much that an all-expenses-paid shopping spree can get me that I can't get myself.

"Even better." Annika smiles at us, one by one by one. "You may each ask me a single question."

The piano music seems to grow louder as we fall silent.

"What kind of question?" Lemon asks a moment later.

Annika shrugs. "Any kind. About whatever you want. Me, your teachers, other students, troublemaking in general. I reserve the right to answer as I please, but the questions are wide open."

Gabby's hand shoots up.

"Yes?" Annika says.

Gabby's hand drops back to the table. "Has anyone ever been killed?"

I've just taken the last sip of cider; it burns as I force it down my throat. Before I can start choking, I grab my water glass and drink some more.

"You mean like a student?" Annika asks. "During training?"

Gabby nods.

"No. Next?"

That's it? What about *not* during training? I'd ask, but I don't want to waste my question.

"I have one," Lemon says. "What do you think is the best talent a Troublemaker can have?"

Annika takes a forkful of salad and chews thoughtfully. Several seconds later she swallows and says, "Patience."

"That's not a talent," Abe says.

"If you had more of it, maybe you wouldn't be so quick to

disagree." Annika turns toward Lemon. "It doesn't matter what your talent is. What matters is how you use it. Doing so intelligently and effectively requires knowing risks, outcomes, and potential consequences. Knowing those requires patience."

I consider this as I eat my fish sticks—which, not for nothing, are even moister and sweeter than the ones in the Kanteen. Before I can assess my own patience level, Abe raises his hand.

"Go ahead," Annika says.

"You said we could ask about other Troublemakers, right?"

"Right."

"Good. Because there's one question I've been dying to know the answer to for weeks."

This is followed by a pause. It lasts so long I look up . . . and see Abe grinning at me.

"If Kilter's so competitive," he says, still grinning, "and if you only accept a certain number of kids each year . . . why'd you take Hinkle a month into the semester?"

I jump up. The back of my chair hits the chest of my waiter, who stumbles backward.

"Sorry," I say. Then, "Bathroom?"

"Allow me," my waiter says.

"That's okay. I'll find it."

I dash around the table and through the door before anyone can say anything else. Between the water and cider I do have to use the bathroom, but more importantly, I don't want to hear Annika answer Abe's question. To put as much space between them and me as possible, as if that will make a difference, I follow the hallway we took to one we didn't, take that to a wide staircase, charge to the second floor, and dart into the first room I come to.

Inside, I shut my eyes and rest my forehead on the closed door. When my breathing slows, I turn around and see I didn't find a bathroom after all. I found a bedroom. With white furniture. Flowered wallpaper. A pink bedspread and purple pillows. Dozens of stuffed animals. It'd be a typical girl's room if the windows weren't covered in sheets, blocking out the light . . . and if everything in it wasn't covered in a thick layer of dust.

Temporarily forgetting why I'm there, I go over to the dresser. It's covered with small porcelain dolls and picture frames. The latter are the only things not caked in a gray film. In the photos, a young Annika rides horses, smiles with friends, and poses with her family.

At least, I assume it's her family. There's Annika, another girl whose face is partially hidden by a baseball cap, a pretty woman . . . and a decapitated man. His arms are around the girls, but his head has been ripped from the picture.

Stuck in the corner of the frame is a newspaper clipping. I lean in closer for a better look.

Following a long illness, Lucelia Kilter, 38, passed away at her family's home in Mount Collins, New York. She is survived by her husband, Maximus, and two daughters: Annika, 12, and Nadia, 10.

"You missed."

I spin around. My waiter stands in the open doorway.

"The bathroom's one door down."

"Oh. Right."

I hurry into the hallway, find the bathroom, and take care of business. As I follow the waiter back downstairs, my mind struggles with two thoughts.

The first is that Annika was my age when she lost her mother.

The second is that I hope Capital T was listening when

Annika said patience was the best talent a Troublemaker could have. Because I'll need theirs if I'm going to explain my side of what she told them while I was gone.

Reaching the dining room, I keep my head lowered as I return to my seat.

"Everything okay?" Lemon asks quietly.

I open my mouth to say yes, then realize what he just said. If he wants to know if I'm okay . . . does that mean he still cares? Even though he knows the truth about me?

"Are you ready, Seamus?"

I look from Lemon to Annika. She smiles.

"You didn't miss anything, if that's what you're wondering. I chose not to answer Abe, so now it's your turn."

I sneak a quick peek across the table. Gabby eats and listens. Abe picks at his mashed potatoes. Neither looks like they've just learned they're having dinner with a cold-blooded killer.

"Seamus," Annika says gently. "Do you have a question?"

I turn back and give her a small smile. Partly because I'm sad for her, partly because I'm grateful, and mostly because I just learned a lot without asking anything at all.

"Yes," I say. "Are there any more fish sticks?"

Chapter 21

DEMERITS: 1950
GOLD STARS: 180

Dude," Lemon says. "Looking sharp."

I stand before the full-length mirror and tighten my tie. My reflection shoots him a quick smile. "You too."

It's Parents' Day. I'm wearing my navy-blue suit. He's wearing jeans, a tucked-in, button-down shirt, and real shoes with laces. For Lemon, this is formal attire.

"Nervous?" he asks.

"A little. You?"

"Terrified." He takes a lighter from the desk, puts it down, and picks it up again. Fortunately, there's a knock on the door, giving him something to do.

Figuring it's Gabby and Abe stopping by so we can walk together, I go into the bathroom to brush my teeth for the third time since breakfast. I'm just about to spit when Lemon appears in the doorway with two packages. One's open, the other's not.

"More presents, and Christmas is still three weeks away." He holds up the open package. Inside are gray flannel pants and a matching short-sleeved shirt wrapped in a shiny silver ribbon. "There's a card, too." He holds it up and reads. "'Dear Trouble-makers. Enclosed please find your required outfit for today's events. It's not fancy, but it's super comfortable—and will help reassure your parents that you're here for the right reasons. Thank you in advance for your cooperation. See you soon. xoxo, Annika.'"

I spit and rinse.

"What do you think?" Lemon asks. "Skip the pajamas and stick with street threads? Maybe earn a few extra demerits?"

"It's probably not a good day for defying authority," I say. "We don't want our parents to think Kilter's not working and take us out, do we?"

"Good point." He leaves my box on the counter and returns to the bedroom.

As I change, I think about what I just said. For a long time, all I wanted was to talk to my parents, to hear their voices. Now I'm excited to see them . . . but I'm scared, too. A lot's happened since my call home on Thanksgiving, but after replaying the one-sided conversation in my head a million times, I can still hear every word, laugh, and musical note like it took place yesterday. And despite my recent troublemaking accomplishments, that memory and old questions rushed back as soon as my alarm went off this morning.

Like, what if they're still mad at me? What if they're so mad, they don't even come? Worse, what if they're so mad they *do* come—but bring Bartholomew John with them? To try to get me to feel as bad as they do?

Only one scenario would be worse than that, and that's if they're not here because they've already forgotten about their criminal son and moved on. This would confirm what that phone call suggested.

I try not to think about it as I finish getting ready and Lemon and I head to the Kilter Arena, which is a fancy name for the tent, bleachers, and planks of wood Kilter maintenance set up far away from the rest of campus for today's festivities. I feel okay until we reach the main gate, and then I suddenly can't feel my legs. I stop before the entrance and stand there, paralyzed.

"Seamus?" Lemon stops next to me.

"I'm okay. I just need a minute."

He gives me that plus several seconds. Then he tries again. "You're a good friend."

I look at him. "What?"

His shoulders lift. "You put up with my weird fire obsession. You worry about me when I sleepwalk. You stay calm when Abe and Gabby freak out. You totally rocked it with Mystery." His shoulders drop. "You're a good friend. I wanted you to know that before we went in there."

Now, I have friends back home. Not many, and not the kind you have sleepovers with, but two or three of the kind you could sit next to on the bus, or talk to in the softball outfield during gym. But I've never been through anything with them like what I've been through with Lemon. After all, it's not every day that you attack your teacher, are attacked by your teacher, potentially endanger the lives of your classmates . . . and then earn praise and prizes for your efforts.

At Kilter, this is the stuff friendships are built on.

"Thanks," I say. "So are you."

This exchange gives us both enough strength to enter the arena. The presentation hasn't started yet, and our classmates and their families are scattered throughout the bleachers. I spot Abe sitting with his parents; he talks nonstop to his mother, who separates him from his stepfather, who's staring at the stage. Gabby sits between her parents two bleachers up. Her mother's doing the talking in their family, pausing every few seconds to brush her hair or check her appearance in a compact mirror. When Gabby tries to speak, her mother pats her knee and talks over her, and her dad's arm tightens around her.

"There are Ziggy and Babs." Lemon nods to a couple sitting on the lawn next to the bleachers. His dad looks just like him but with a beard and lower slouch. His mom's about two feet shorter and has long, dark hair—and a very round belly.

"She's having a baby?" I ask.

"Any second now." Lemon bumps my arm with his fist. "Good luck. I'll find you later."

I watch him join them. His mom climbs to her knees and embraces him in a huge hug. As she squeezes, his dad shakes his hand and pats his head. They're clearly happy to see him, which encourages me to look for my own parents.

I do a lap around the arena. Not spotting them, I do a second. I'm nearing the entrance for the third time and worrying they didn't come when I hear a familiar voice.

Heart thumping, I follow the voice to the wide aisle that separates the two sets of bleachers and leads to the stage. I take one step forward and then stop.

Because I see her. My mother. But instead of sitting in the bleachers like everyone else's parents, she's on the stage with the Kilter faculty, talking to Annika . . . and laughing.

"Sport!"

Two arms fly around my shoulders and squeeze so tightly my feet lift off the ground.

"It's great to see you! Have you gotten taller? You look taller!"

I look away from the stage and pat the chubby hands clamped on my triceps. When they let go, I turn around and throw my arms around Dad. My eyes water as we hug. I wait for them to dry again before pulling away.

"Hi, Dad."

"Hey, kiddo." As he tousles my hair, I see his eyes water too. "You look good. Are you good?"

"I'm fine." Which, now that I know he's happy to see me, has never been truer. "How are you?"

"Great!" He claps his hands to his belly. "And five pounds lighter, thanks to your mom's new—"

"Hello, Seamus."

I'm pretty sure my heart stops, but somehow I manage to turn around. "Mom. Hi."

She's standing in the aisle, wearing a pretty red coat and matching heels. Her hair has been cut and lightened. She wears lipstick, which I notice because she never wears makeup—and also because her lips are set in a thin, straight line.

She's mad. Disappointed. Furious. She might've just been laughing with Annika, but she's still upset that her son could do something as terrible as what I did to Miss Parsippany.

"I've missed you," she says.

Her lips curve in a wide smile, and she pulls me into a big hug. Dad throws his arms around both of us. We stand there like a Hinkle sandwich until Annika asks everyone to take their seats.

"I hear you're doing a wonderful job," Mom whispers as we sit down. "That makes me very happy."

She's not mad. She's not sad or disappointed. She's *happy.* I can't remember the last time I did something that made her feel that way. It's so nice to hear, I decide to put off asking about Bartholomew John.

The presentation, which has been carefully crafted for parental viewing, begins. The Kilter faculty and staff are dressed in military-green pantsuits and tall boots like the ones Annika wore the first time we met. She's wearing them too. They all sit in metal folding chairs behind a podium. Upperclassmen speak about all the bad things they did before Kilter and all the wonderful things they've done since beginning Kilter. Houdini, Fern, Wyatt, and our other teachers talk about the importance of structure and discipline and respect for one's elders. They're all serious, solemn. I'm sure there's not a parent in the arena who'd guess that Fern has a high-tech whoopee cushion strapped to her calf.

I only half listen to the presentation. I'm too busy sneaking glances at Mom, who holds my hand and smiles at the stage like it's filled with dancing clowns instead of reform-school personnel, and at Dad, who only lifts his arm from around my shoulders to pat my head whenever someone refers to "your well-behaved child." And I'm thinking maybe, just maybe, this will all turn out okay. I'll do what I have to here, spend some more QT with my good friend Lemon, and smooth things over with Elinor. Then I'll go home, where Mom, Dad, and I will talk more and be closer than we ever were.

And eventually, when we look back at the cafeteria incident, maybe we won't just remember it as a terrible, horrible event that ruined our lives. Maybe we'll remember it as a terrible, horrible event that *changed* our lives—for the better.

The thought leaves me so hopeful I practically skip along the tour that follows the presentation. This is really saying something, because Annika doesn't lead us through the gardens and sleek, shiny buildings I've come to know so well. Instead she takes us down a dark, underground tunnel that leads from a patch of grass near the arena to a patch of dirt a half mile away. When we climb out, we're in the grassless front yard of an old building I've never seen before. It resembles the administrative building we entered that first day, except it's bigger and scarier. Outside, barbed wire crisscrosses the yard like garland on a Christmas tree. Iron bars block clouded windows. Gray dogs with big muscles and sharp teeth growl at us from behind a chain-link fence.

Inside, there's no natural light. The small common areas contain minimal furniture and no TVs or entertainment of any kind. The classrooms have wooden desks and chairs and chalkboards filled with lessons on discipline and respect. The sleeping wing has two large rooms, one for boys and one for girls, with mattresses covering the floors. The mattresses are made up with gray sheets and flat pillows to give the appearance that people actually sleep there.

Most parents, disturbed by the fake living conditions, pull their kids closer as we walk. Dad tries the same with me, but I assure him I'm fine and smile to prove it.

The tour ends in a large room, where card tables and metal folding chairs are arranged around two indoor grills. A windowless door that leads outside is open for ventilation. The tables are covered in red-checkered tablecloths and decorated with vases holding a single daisy each. Devin and Houdini cook, and the rest of the faculty and staff excuse themselves, presumably to give the families some time alone.

"Seamus, over here!"

I spot Lemon and his parents across the room. He's dragging two card tables to a third to make one long one. Gabby and Abe are dragging chairs.

"Want to meet my friends?" I ask Mom and Dad.

"Friends?" Mom beams. "Nothing would make us happier."

There it is again. Happiness. Who knew a thing like that would come from a place like this?

Introductions are made. Everyone sits. Small talk ensues. Oldies music streams from a radio Devin sets up on the floor. Soon the lunch feels almost festive, and people relax enough to joke and laugh.

"Seamus," Mom says at one point, "will you please find me some more ketchup?"

"You got it." I jump up. "Anyone need anything else?"

No one does. As I hurry away, I hear Babs, Lemon's mom, comment on what a polite son Mom and Dad have.

Devin tells me extra ketchup's in the fake kitchen. I run down a long, dark hall, trying to remember where the room was on the tour. Reaching a dead end, I turn around—and stop short to keep from running into Elinor.

"Hi," I say.

"Hi," she says.

I think she'll run away again, but she doesn't. She holds up her book and offers a small smile.

"I was just looking for a quiet place to read."

"Oh. Did your parents have to leave early?" I ask, remembering the photo Elinor left in the gazebo. This is the first time we've talked since then, so I haven't had a chance to ask what she was doing with the picture—or who the young woman with copper eyes is. Is she Elinor's mother? And if so, what was she doing with Annika? Were they childhood friends? Are they still friends? Is that why Annika expects more from Elinor?

"Yes," Elinor says after a pause. "My dad had to work."

I've been having such a nice day with my parents that this makes me feel even worse for her than I normally would. I instantly forget all my other questions.

"But I'm fine," she says. "Totally. This just gives me more time to catch up on my reading."

"Okay." I debate whether to say what I'm about to say, then decide I have nothing to lose. "I'm here, you know."

Her eyes meet mine. "I know. I see you."

"No, I mean . . . I'm *here*. Like, as a friend. If you ever want to hang out, or talk, or not talk, or whatever. You can take me up on it now, later, or never. But I wanted you to know."

She studies me, maybe to see if I'm serious. "Okay," she finally says. "Thank you."

"You're welcome." I smile. She steps aside so I can pass. I'm halfway down the hall when she calls after me.

"They didn't come."

I stop.

"My parents." Her voice is louder, brighter. "They didn't think a seven-hour flight was worth a three-hour visit. So they didn't come."

This is the most personal information she's shared since we've been here. I'm tempted to ride the wave of openness and ask about the picture from the gazebo, but quickly decide not to push it. There will be time for that later.

I turn around. "Would you like to have lunch with us?"

She nods, her cheeks turning pink.

Together, we find the kitchen and the ketchup and head back to the makeshift dining room. The talking and laughter has escalated, and with my parents here and Elinor by my side, I'm thinking this day can't get any better.

Until we near our table. And I hear what everyone's talking about.

"An apple?" Mrs. Ryan says.

"An apple," Mom says.

"One hit?" Mr. Hansen says.

"One hit," Mom says.

"Judith," Dad says quietly, "maybe now's not the best time to—"

"It's the perfect time! Our kid's doing well. *All* of our kids are doing well. Why hide the enormous obstacles they had to overcome?"

I sneak a peek at Elinor. She looks at Mom, then at me, then Mom again.

"So as I was saying, the substitute teacher was in the middle of the brawl. Seamus, confused and angry and scared all at once, picked up the only weapon he could find and hurled it straight across the cafeteria. The apple got her in the head, and that was it." Mom takes a big bite of her burger. "She was a goner, and my Seamus was a criminal."

The noise from the other tables grows louder as ours falls silent.

"Let me get this straight," Lemon says a moment later. "Seamus threw an apple at his substitute teacher . . . and she *died*?"

Mom swallows. "Yup."

"So he killed her?"

She licks her fingers. "Indeed."

"And that's the reason he's here?"

She picks her teeth. "The one and only."

Lemon looks at me. Gabby and Abe look at me. Their parents try not to but look at me anyway. Elinor takes one more look at me before walking, then running, away.

No one says anything. They don't have to.

I force my feet to move toward the table. I place the ketchup gently by Mom's plate.

"I'm sorry," I say.

And then I leave.

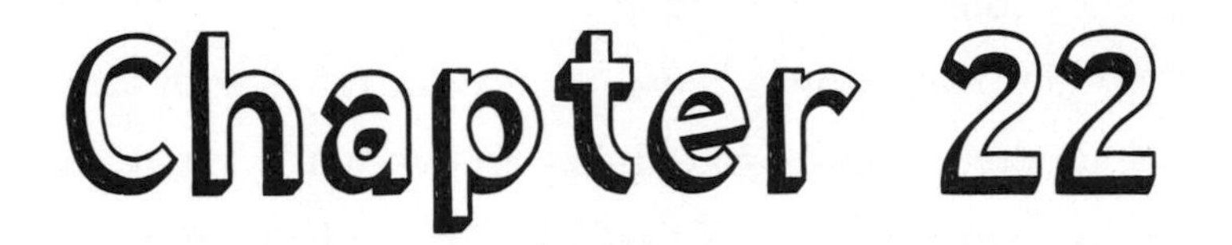

DEMERITS: 2201
GOLD STARS: 180

TO: parsippany@cloudviewschools.net
FROM: shinkle@kilteracademy.org
SUBJECT: Alone in a Crowded Cafeteria

Dear Miss Parsippany,

I've thought a lot about how you must've felt in the cafeteria that day. Nervous. Excited. Scared. But it occurred to me recently that you might've felt something else, too.

Lonely.

When you walked into a room filled with two hundred people you didn't know but wanted to like you, you must've felt this more than anything else. And the fight only made it worse. Because if kids and teachers saw you there and you didn't try to help, you would've become the wimpy substitute who didn't care. If you tried to help and failed, you would've become the wacky substitute with delusions of strength and grandeur. If you tried to help and succeeded, you might've become the school's first cool substitute . . . but Bartholomew John alone had fifty pounds on you, so what were the chances of that? No matter what, you were going to be judged by people who didn't know you, and that had to make you feel like you were totally on your own.

Which is exactly how I've been feeling lately. On Parents' Day, after Mom spilled the beans about what I did, I was kicked out of Capital T. No one told me so, but I figured as much when Lemon, Abe, and Gabby stopped talking to me. I haven't been to a single meeting since and they haven't come looking for me, so I'm pretty sure I'm right. Lemon ignores me in our room, and even worse, he's stopped playing with matches there. Which means he's either kicked the habit (doubtful), or he no longer trusts me around fire (likely). I never thought I'd want to wake up to raging flames, but guess what? Now I do.

And then there's Elinor. She doesn't talk to me either, though I catch her looking at me every now and then. I can only imagine what she's thinking—and whatever it is, I don't blame her. I lied. I didn't lie when I said I was there for her, but who wants a cold-blooded killer for a friend?

My teachers act like nothing has happened, and to them, nothing has. They already knew the truth. Unlike my classmates, the rest of whom quickly heard about what I did and immediately kept their distance, my teachers thought it was one of my better qualities.

Now I have only one option: to lie low until it's time to leave. I'd try getting kicked out, except I'm in no hurry to go home. Instead I complete my assignments, read, and watch TV. It's not exciting, but it's all I have.

Anyway, I just wanted to say I understand. About the loneliness. And that I'm sorry, again, for everything. Wherever you are, I hope you're happier than you were that day in the cafeteria.

Sincerely,

Seamus Hinkle

Then, before I can change my mind, I write another note.

TO: loliver@kilteracademy.org
FROM: shinkle@kilteracademy.org
SUBJECT: Dinner

Hi Lemon,

You probably already have plans, but if not, do you want to have dinner together tonight? It'd be nice to catch up. Maybe explain some things.

Let me know.

—Seam

I don't finish my name. The glass door I'm leaning against opens. I fall back and drop my K-Pak.

"That must be some worm," Martin, the Kommissary cashier, says.

"Sorry?" I jump up. Pick up the K-Pak. Shake it when the screen's scrambled.

"It's barely nine a.m. That makes you the early bird. Whatever you're hoping to buy is the worm."

The K-Pak screen blinks, then clears, returning to the main menu instead of K-Mail. Relieved that I didn't break anything, I put the computer in my backpack and follow Martin inside.

"It is," I say. "Some worm, that is."

He moves through the store, turning on lights and unlocking display cases. I put my hand on the print pad and wait for the greeting.

WELCOME, SEAMUS HINKLE! YOU HAVE . . . 2,001 CREDITS!

The turnstile beeps. I push through.

"So, what'll it be?" Martin asks. "Paintball pellets? New bows and arrows? A titanium Boomaree?"

A titanium Boomaree? I didn't know they made those. For

a split second I'm tempted to ask to see one, but then I remind myself why I'm there.

"The Kilter Smoke Detector with Automatic Flame Eliminator," I say. "Please."

He's straightening a stack of camouflage T-shirts. At my request, he stops and looks up.

"That's two thousand credits," he says.

"I know."

"How many do you have?"

"Two thousand and one."

"How are you going to buy more supplies?"

I shrug. "I guess I won't."

He considers this, then takes a large key ring from the belt loop of his pants and starts for the back of the store. "Whatever you say, hotshot. I just work here."

I wait by the counter. A minute later he appears carrying a clear plastic box. The thin disc, no bigger than a silver dollar, is inside. The transaction's over in seconds, and then I'm outside again. I slide the box in my backpack for safekeeping and start down the sidewalk.

"Good morning!"

I stop and look to the left, where Annika's sitting in a golf cart.

She wears a silver parka like the one (most) Troublemakers wear, only hers is longer and trimmed in sparkly white fur. A fluffy white bomber hat protects her head. Her eyes are hidden by shiny silver sunglasses.

"It's a cold one." Her breath forms a white cloud, proving her point. "How about a ride?"

The question sparks a quick mental debate. Before Parents' Day I would've climbed right in. But now that I'm Kilter's biggest social outcast? I don't know if I should. Being escorted to math class by the school's director probably won't earn me any popularity points.

"Let's try that again. I'd *like* to give you a ride."

She still smiles, but her tone's serious. Guessing this is more of a demand than a request, I round the cart and get in.

"So, how are things?" she asks, her voice lighter, once we're driving. We travel at a normal, nonwarp speed, making it easier to talk.

"Fine," I say. Then, "Great. Never been better."

She shoots me a look. "Really. Is that why you've been sitting by yourself at meals? Spending your free time in the TV lounge? Staying out of trouble?"

I don't know what to say. So I don't say anything.

"Is it your parents? Do you miss them? There are only a few

days left in the semester, you know. After that you'll get to go home for three whole weeks."

My heart stops. "Three weeks?"

"Yup."

"And then what?"

"And then you report back for the spring semester."

She says this pleasantly, matter-of-factly. Like it's a done deal, something to look forward to. But all I can think is that once I leave, no matter how awkward things might be at home, I'm going to do everything I can to forget I was ever here.

"Great power comes with great responsibility," Annika says a moment later. "Have you heard that before?"

I shake my head.

"It's one of my favorite expressions. It means the more you have to give, the more people expect from you. You have the ability to both please and disappoint in ways others can't, so you must be extremely careful in the choices you make. At the same time, you have to always be thinking about the greater good. It's an exhilarating but difficult position to be in."

I think I understand . . . but I don't know why we're talking about it.

The golf cart stops. Annika faces me.

"It also means there are no friends at the top. And, Seamus, that's where you are."

Technically, we're outside the classroom building . . . but she's not speaking geographically. If she's referring to class rankings, which is my next guess, this still doesn't make sense. I haven't checked them lately, but she's right: I've barely made any trouble since Parents' Day. Lemon should be at the top—and he has friends. One less than he used to, but still.

Before I can say any of this, Annika steps out of the cart and nods to the building.

"Shall we? I have some administrative business to take care of."

I shuffle after her. In the classroom, I take my new seat in the otherwise unoccupied front row, and Annika heads for Houdini. He's sleeping with his head on the desk, the hood of his orange sweatshirt pulled past his nose. Annika lifts the hood with one finger. Houdini reels back from the light like it comes from lasers shooting directly into his eyes.

"I see we've reached the productivity pilfering section of your lesson plan," she says.

Houdini grumbles, then tries to look more awake. Annika faces the class and smiles.

"Congratulations, Troublemakers. After training hard for

eleven weeks, you're nearing the end of your first Kilter Academy session."

The room explodes into cheers and applause. Annika holds up one hand and waits for the noise to die down.

"The finish line's in sight, but you're not over it yet. Before you continue, you must complete your first Ultimate Troublemaking Task."

"I thought we were done," Abe says, sounding confused. "Once we got all the teachers."

"Not quite," Annika says.

"There's always a final exam," Houdini adds with a yawn.

"And this will be the hardest you've ever had," Annika says. "Only a handful of Troublemakers successfully completes the task each semester."

"What happens to the others?" Gabby asks.

"They enroll in an additional, mandatory one-month training session that makes what you've done so far seem like a joke. If they earn enough demerits during this session, they may rejoin their classmates at the start of the spring semester. If they don't, their Kilter careers will come to an early conclusion."

"You mean they'll get kicked out?" Abe asks.

"Precisely," Annika says.

"And the Troublemakers who do complete the task?" Lemon says. "What happens to them?"

"They automatically advance and earn the opportunity to join the faculty member of their choice in a top secret, real-world combat mission." Her eyes travel from one student to the next. "If they do exceptionally well, they may even choose me."

Excited whispers fill the room. I sneak a peek over my shoulder at Elinor—then spin back when she's looking at me.

"Now I must warn you," Annika says. "This year's task is, by far, the most challenging in the history of first-year Ultimate Troublemaking Tasks. It's so difficult, I wouldn't be surprised if no one completes it."

She aims her K-Pak at the wall behind the desk. A moving image of her as a teenager appears. We're silent as young Annika sits in a window seat piled with pillows and watches the snow fall outside. She's wearing a red velvet dress. Her hair's in a French braid and tied with a red ribbon. The brightly colored lights of a Christmas tree, which must be across the room from her, twinkle in the windowpane.

A minute or so into the video, a woman wearing a black

dress and white apron enters the frame; she offers Annika a cup of tea, which Annika declines. A few minutes after that she brings a blanket, and another minute after that, slippers. Annika shakes her head at both without turning from the window. After another long stretch, the woman enters the frame again. This time she offers Annika a silver cordless phone. Annika looks at it like she's not sure she should take it. She finally does, and says five words over the next thirty seconds.

"Okay." "I understand." "Merry Christmas."

She hands the phone back to the woman, who leaves the frame. Then she gets up and walks toward the camera. Before the image cuts out, we see two things.

A WELCOME HOME! banner hanging above the door next to the window.

And tears running down her face.

Grown-up Annika replaces the K-Pak on her belt and faces us.

"I was fifteen when that video was taken. I'm thirty-eight now." She pauses, her expression blank. "And I haven't cried in twenty-three years."

"That's not—"

Annika turns not one, but two evil eyes on Elinor. Elinor

stops speaking instantly. Probably because the death stare burns the words right out of her head.

If she'd been able to finish her sentence, I assume Elinor would've said that's not true—that Annika *has* cried since she was fifteen years old. And I can't help thinking a person would have to be very close to our friendly-yet-somewhat-detached director to know this.

"Your Ultimate Troublemaking Task," Annika continues, "should you choose to accept it, is to change that. Make me cry, sob, weep, what have you. The goal is to get real tears sliding down these cheeks."

This is met with silence. I wonder if she's serious. Apparently, so do my classmates.

"How?" Lemon finally asks.

Annika laughs. "If I knew that, this wouldn't be the most challenging task in the history of first-year tasks, would it?"

"Can we . . . hurt you?" Abe asks, like the question alone might do it. "Physically, I mean?"

"I draw the line at knives and guns, but our security's such that I know I don't have to worry about that. Everything else is fair game." She places her hands on Houdini's desk and leans toward us. "You should know I'm tougher than I look."

"That's no lie," Houdini confirms.

"You have five days," she says, striding toward the door. "Good luck!"

Personally, I think this is an *Unfortunate* Troublemaking Task. My classmates, however, don't agree. They're so excited, Houdini gives up trying to get us to focus on stealing and lets us plan our attacks. As he puts his head back on his desk, I take out my K-Pak. I'm about to start another note to Miss Parsippany when I catch two words that everyone else is too distracted to hear.

"Annika's Apex."

I turn slowly in my seat, dreading what I see before I see it.

Lemon, Abe, and Gabby are huddled together in the back of the room. Abe makes a T with his pointer fingers, then slides one finger down and connects the tips of his thumbs to make a triangle. He lowers the triangle in front of the tall flame coming from the mouth of a lighter that Lemon holds.

We might not have hung out lately, but I've spent enough time with Capital T to know immediately what this means.

Annika's childhood amusement park.

They're going to destroy it.

Chapter 23

DEMERITS: 2201
GOLD STARS: 180

Later that night, I can't sit still. I move from my bed to my desk chair. From my desk chair to the floor. From the floor to the windowsill. From the windowsill back to my bed. As I move, my eyes travel from the wall clock to the door to Lemon's pillow, where my last-chance peace offering rests. When the door finally opens, I'm so nervous—and excited—I practically leap across the room.

And Lemon steps back into the hallway.

"Sorry." I step back too and hold up both hands so he can see they're empty. "I'm sorry. Come in. Please."

He does. Warily. He gives the room a once-over as he passes through the doorway, like I might've rigged it with automatic weapons while he was gone, and then heads for his bed. When he reaches the pillow, he stops short.

"What's that?"

I force my feet to stay put. "A present."

His back is to me. I wait for him to take the package from the pillow, but he doesn't. He simply stares down at it without moving.

"Don't you want to open it?"

He's still for several more seconds. I'm thinking I should've saved the receipt, when he slowly reaches forward and picks it up. He keeps his back to me as he unties the silver shoelace I used for a ribbon and opens the spare trash-can liner I used for wrapping paper.

I hold my breath. Brace for his response.

"Dude," he says with a sigh.

"It's the Kilter Smoke Detector with Automatic Flame Eliminator." The words fly from my mouth.

"I know what it is." He turns around. "I just don't know why you bought it."

"Because you wanted it."

"Yes, but—"

"And because I'm sorry." I step toward him, heart racing. "I'm so sorry, Lemon, for not telling you the truth. I was just so scared of what you'd think of me if you knew what I did, I couldn't tell you. I could barely tell myself. But you're my roommate. My friend. You deserved to know, and I should've told you."

His eyes lower to the gift. The rest of him lowers to the edge of his bed. "It's not just that. I understand why you didn't want to tell me."

I pause. "Then what is it?"

He frowns. "Seamus, what I do, what other Troublemakers here do . . . it's not like what you do."

"What I *did*. One time. By accident."

"Even so." His eyes meet mine. "You're in a totally different league."

I shake my head, take another step toward him. "Can I at least explain what happened that day? So you know exactly why I did what I did? And that I didn't mean to hurt anyone?"

"Will the story end the same way?"

I open my mouth. Close it. Try again. "Well, yes. I can't change the past."

"Then I don't think you can change the future, either."

He sounds sorry as he says this, and I almost expect him to take it back, to give me a small smile and ask me to explain away . . . but he doesn't. He stands. Places the gift on his bed. Takes some clothes from his dresser and puts them in his backpack. And shuffles toward the door.

"Where are you going?"

He stops with one hand on the doorknob. "I'm crashing at Abe's tonight. We've got some work to do, so . . ."

"Can I come?" I'd cringe at the desperation in my voice if I weren't so desperate. "I know what you want to do to Annika's Apex. I can help."

He pauses. When he speaks again, there's a slight edge to his voice. "If you want to help, see if you can convince the Kommissary to break its no-returns rule and take back the smoke detector. We could use the credits to buy supplies."

Now I cringe. The rejection of my peace offering stings. It almost makes me miss the rest of what he just said.

"What happened to your credits?" I don't remember exact

numbers, but we were all fairly loaded after taking down Mr. Tempest.

"Gone. We thought we were done after Mystery, so we blew them on scooters. Now we have no choice but to beg, borrow, and steal equipment for the Ultimate Troublemaking Task."

And with that, he opens the door and leaves.

I stand there, numb. Then I run after him.

"Lemon! Wait!"

But I'm too late. He's already gone. The only people in the hallway are two Good Samaritans; they tip invisible hats at me and continue to the exit. As they head outside, the second Good Samaritan's red fanny pack catches on the door. He does a little wiggle to release it . . . and I get an idea.

The Good Samaritans' job is to stop trouble, no matter how big or how small. Two months ago, when they stormed our room to put out Lemon's fire, they were armed with extinguishers, smoke vacuums, and other equipment. And if they use that much equipment to take care of one minor dorm-room emergency . . . what do they use for something more serious?

According to the Kommissary Krew's last e-mail, which they sent while I was in math class learning about the Ultimate

Troublemaking Task, I have one credit left. So if I want more weapons, I'm going to have to get them another way.

I bolt into my room, grab my boots and jacket, and throw them on as I dash down the hall.

There are no friends at the top.

You can't change the future.

Determined to prove both Annika and Lemon wrong, I move faster. Outside, I catch up with the Good Samaritans quickly and then follow them at a safe distance.

For the next hour, I run, hide behind bushes and trees, and listen to some really boring conversations about lawn care and car maintenance. Eventually, the Good Samaritans head for a part of campus I've never seen before. They stop at a bike rack to pick up an electric, two-person bicycle, and zoom into the woods. I follow on foot. Moonlight illuminates the tire tracks, which I use as my guide.

About a mile in, the tracks end at the bicycle itself. It's parked in a small, empty clearing. There are no buildings. There are also no Good Samaritans. Certain it's a trap with a hidden lasso that's about to grab my ankle and turn me upside down, I back up slowly.

I'm at the edge of the clearing when the ground begins to shake. The tall pine trees sway. The red bicycle bounces like it's flying down a rocky mountain trail.

And a wide, silver cylinder rises up from the dirt.

I dart behind a cluster of rocks and drop to my knees. Holding my breath, I watch the cylinder rotate, then stop. A door slides open, and three Good Samaritans step out. Two climb on the red bicycle, and the third unfolds a standing scooter he's brought with him from wherever they were. They shoot off in the same direction—away from me—just as the cylinder door starts to slide shut.

I fly from my hiding spot and toward that cylinder like the Good Samaritans are chasing me. And maybe they are. I'm not about to waste one second looking behind me to find out.

I reach the cylinder and squeeze through the remaining narrow space. The door slides closed. There's a loud beeping, like the sound a garbage truck makes backing up, and then a steady hum as the steel elevator begins its descent.

I hardly hear the noises over my thundering heart.

"You were taking a walk and got lost," I whisper. "You were looking for some upper-level Troublemakers you followed into the woods and found this instead. You had a really good idea for controlling pesky weeds and—"

"Hoodlum Hotline, how may I direct your call?"

The steel door slides open. A middle-aged woman with bright orange hair and long fake nails appears. A three-legged Chihuahua sleeps in a bed on her desk. She's talking and typing and doesn't look up from the computer screen as I step out of the cylinder and fly around the corner.

If we were aboveground, I'd stop and say hello to Ms. Marla. But here, I don't want to push my luck—which, for perhaps the first time ever, is on my side.

Because it's seven o'clock. And in the Good Samaritan secret bunker, that's dinnertime.

They're gathered around a table filled with Crock-Pots and casserole dishes in a large dining room. I tiptoe past the open doorway, though they're so busy loading their plates I could knock and they wouldn't notice. I hurry down the long white hallway and stop by a door labeled GS LOCKER ROOM ONE. When I don't hear anything, I open the door and step inside.

It looks a lot like the boys' locker room at Cloudview. The walls are lined with regular metal lockers. Benches sit before the lockers.

There's a water fountain. A bathroom with stalls and showers.

There's just one thing this locker room has that Cloudview's doesn't: an enormous closet filled with khaki pants, checkered shirts, sports coats, and penny loafers.

I run in, grab the smallest size of each, and shove them into my backpack. Returning to the main room, I lunge for the door—and stop with one hand on the knob.

As it happens, there are actually two things this locker room has that Cloudview's doesn't. The first is the closet.

The second is a "WANTED" poster.

It hangs on the wall by the door and contains twelve color photos. Eleven are of kids I don't recall seeing at Kilter; they're wanted for things like blackmail and armed robbery.

The twelfth photo is of a woman. She appears to be in her early thirties and has reddish hair and brownish eyes. She's not smiling, but even so, she looks like an older version of the girl in the picture with Annika—the one Elinor dropped in the gazebo a few weeks ago.

Which reminds me. If I really want to repair our friendship, I should probably return that.

I step closer to read the name beneath the photo.

Nadia Kilter.

I step back. The woman with copper eyes isn't just Annika's friend; she's Annika's sister. And if I'm right, if the woman is also Elinor's mother . . . that means Annika is Elinor's aunt.

This realization is so startling it takes me a second to wonder what Nadia did to make it onto that poster.

"Those were the best Swedish meatballs I've ever had."

"How about the chicken parm? Finger-lickin' heaven!"

The male voices come from the hallway. They get louder, then softer. Forgetting the poster for now, I crack open the door to make sure they're heading toward the Hoodlum Hotline desk, and then I slip out and run in the opposite direction.

I'm pretty sure pressing my luck will guarantee losing it, so I follow the hallway all the way to the end and duck into an unmarked room to wait out dessert. After their visit to our room, Lemon did some investigating on the Good Samaritans and learned that they work on two shifts: day and night. Once the night shift starts and the place clears out, I'll make my exit.

This room's dark. Cold. Heart racing, I feel along the concrete wall with both hands for a light switch. Not finding one, I yank my K-Pak from my backpack and turn it on.

The screen light's not bright, but it still illuminates electric bicycles. Scooters. Skateboards. Face masks. Wet suits. Paint remover. Oxygen tanks. Garden hoses. Wire spools. Rope balls. Duct tape. Flashlights. Helium tanks. Pool nets. Fire extinguishers. Smoke vacuums.

And every other imaginable supply a Troublemaker could need.

"Bingo," I say.

"Indeed," a Good Samaritan says.

Chapter 24

DEMERITS: 3000
GOLD STARS: 820

Thank you for calling the Hoodlum Hotline, how may I—"

"Hi, Ms. Marla."

There's a pause. "Hello, Seamus."

"Have you found it?"

Another pause. "What?"

"'Ornery.' In your word search. You were having a hard time finding it the last time we talked."

"Not yet. But if you keep calling like this, I might find it in real life."

I try to laugh. Ms. Marla doesn't.

"Sorry," I say. "There's just no one here to talk to. And the GS don't come with lunch for another three hours."

"Well, they don't call it solitary confinement for nothing."

I look around the room that's been home for the past four days. "No, I suppose not."

"Why don't you throw some footballs? Shoot some hoops? Punch out some guards?"

"Excuse me?"

"Video games. I took a tour of the holding cell once. I know you've got more to play with than a Toys 'R' Us."

She's right. There's a lot to do here, like play video games. Watch movies. Read. Swim against the current in a mini lap pool. Make sundaes at the superstocked ice cream bar.

There's just one problem.

I don't feel like doing any of it.

"I have to run," Ms. Marla says. "Personal phone calls aren't really in my job description, if you know what I mean. But chin up. There are only two days left in the semester. After that you're home free."

I thank her, and we hang up. Then, immediately restless, I stand and make the bed, which is twice the size of my dorm-room bed and ten times more comfortable. I take a bath in the marble tub and try to watch the cartoon playing on the flat-screen hanging on the marble wall. I get dressed and comb my hair. I flop on the soft leather couch and consider starting a movie, but then stare at the ceiling instead.

I've been doing a lot of that lately. Staring at the ceiling. Mentally replaying what happened after I was busted in the Good Samaritan supply closet.

There was a lot of confusion. Apparently, I was the very first Troublemaker to break into GS headquarters, and they didn't know what to do with me. They left me with Ms. Marla, who gave me Crock-Pot leftovers and my own word-search book, while they holed up in a conference room to figure it out. Two Good Samaritans eventually returned, grim-faced, and said that they'd discussed my punishment with Annika. Because of the seriousness of my crime, they couldn't simply dock my trouble-making privileges the way they usually did. I couldn't be trusted not to ignore that punishment and make trouble anyway. No, I had to be completely restricted and removed from all temptation.

In solitary confinement. Which, at Kilter, is like the most luxurious hotel suite you can imagine—and never leave.

My K-Pak's on the coffee table. I was surprised the GS didn't confiscate it—at least, until I saw where I'd be staying. And I've been happy to have it. No one sends me direct messages, but I still get the ones all students do, about Kommissary sales and Kanteen menu updates and end-of-semester logistics. They help me feel connected to the rest of the world.

I checked my K-Mail right before calling Ms. Marla, but now I check it again anyway. There's only one new message.

TO: shinkle@kilteracademy.org
FROM: kommissary@kilteracademy.org
SUBJECT: Gold Star Galaxy

Seamus! What's happening?

Seriously. WHAT is happening? Each time we check our records, you've added another constellation of gold stars to your troublemaking sky, which is already pretty full. Rumor has it you're locked up . . . but rumor also has it that there are, like, a million and one things to do there that are a million and one times more fun than calling the Hoodlum

Hotline. Was your holding cell robbed? Is that why you have Marla on speed dial?

Anyway, as you already know, you got 700 demerits for breaking into the Good Samaritans' headquarters, 10 for your weekly allowance, and another few for completing some written class assignments. Your current total is 3000. This is an impressive number, but unfortunately, after adding your most recent Hotline call to the dozens made before it, you have 830 gold stars. Subtract gold stars from demerits, and you have 2170 credits. This is also an impressive number, except now we have to subtract the cost of your previous purchases (Kilter Pocket Extinguisher, 20 credits; Kilter Smoke Detector with Automatic Flame Eliminator, 2000 credits). Do some more math . . . and you've got 150 credits left.

You can still afford a few things at the Kommissary, like miniature Hydra-Bombs and Spiral Spitball Straws with Sticky Pellets, but you can't order them online and we don't deliver. Given your recent phone habits, you might not have any credits left by the time you can stop by in person, so we suggest popping in a few movies to keep you distracted and off the horn.

Unless, of course, you want to be an astronomer instead of a Troublemaker. In which case, dial away and watch those stars shine.

At Your Service,

The Kommissary Krew

I close the note, rest the K-Pak on my chest, and resume staring at the ceiling. A few seconds later, I lift it and start typing.

TO: enorris@kilteracademy.org
FROM: shinkle@kilteracademy.org
SUBJECT: A Prisoner's Apology

Dear Elinor,

You know how, in movies, when the bad guy gets locked up he has a whole lot of time to think about all the terrible things he's done? And how sorry he is for all the pain he's caused? And how, if he had the chance to do it over again, he'd do everything differently? Well, I now know from personal experience that Hollywood didn't make that up. When you're behind bars, this actually happens.

Of course, I thought all those things long before the Good Samaritans whisked me away. But what my sentence has taught me is that I should've done something about them before I couldn't anymore. It's like one of my mom's favorite sayings: Why put off till tomorrow what you can get done today? She usually tosses that one out when I don't get around to cleaning my room or taking out the garbage, but it applies to more serious situations too.

Like apologies. Elinor, when you ran away after hearing the truth on Parents' Day, I should've run too. I should've found you and said I was sorry. Over and over and over. A million times, if that's how much you needed to hear it before you could believe it.

Because I AM sorry. I'm sorry I didn't tell you who I really was. I'm sorry you found out the way you did. I'm sorry you thought you could trust me. I'm sorry I didn't say I was sorry before I was locked up in solitary confinement. Now the semester's ending and I probably won't ever see you again . . . which is sad for a lot of reasons, one being that I'll never get to tell you in person how sorry I am. And how glad I am that we met. And how much I would've liked to be friends.

But at least there's K-Mail, right? It's not perfect, but it's better than nothing.

Have a safe trip home, wherever that is.

Sincerely,

Seamus

I stop. I don't want to mention that I'm not the only one who kept a secret; the fact that Elinor is Annika's niece doesn't exactly compare to the fact that I'm a murderer, and I also want to keep her focused on my apology. But there is something else I'd like to say . . . and knowing what I now do about their relationship, I'm not sure I should. But then I remember how sad Elinor looked that day in the gazebo, and I keep typing.

P.S. Random side note. By now you probably don't care about making Annika happy, but if you want to go out with a bang and prove you're as much a Troublemaker as anyone else here, you might want to talk to Lemon. If they haven't already, he, Abe, and Gabby will bring down Annika's Apex for the Ultimate Troublemaking Task. Last I heard they were out of supplies (and credits) and could use all the help they could get, so they'd probably welcome you with open arms. Just a suggestion.

P.P.S. That was a really long P.S. Sorry!

I reread the note, check for typos. I wait for the doubt, the internal tug of whether I should or shouldn't hit send, but it doesn't come. I have nothing to lose.

So I send it. Then I watch the top of my K-Mail in-box. One minute passes. Five. Ten. Twenty.

No new messages.

I lower the K-Pak and close my eyes. I must drift off, because the next thing I know, I'm hanging off the couch and the Good Samaritans are banging on the door. I catch a glimpse of serious bed-head in the dresser mirror as I run to greet them but ignore it. Surely they've seen worse.

I throw open the door, smile . . . and wish I'd stopped in front of the mirror. Because the Good Samaritans didn't knock.

Elinor did.

"Wow," she says. "When you're sorry, you're *really* sorry."

I swallow, smooth down my hair. "What are you doing here?"

"Taking your mom's advice." She looks at me. When I don't respond right away, she adds, "About not putting things off."

"How did you know where I was?"

"Your note." She shrugs. "And I have my ways."

Her ways? Like top secret familial connections?

Not wanting to push my luck—or make her confess something she'd clearly rather keep to herself—I simply say, "Right."

I nod. She nods. We stand there, not speaking, for a few seconds.

"So should we go?" she finally asks.

"Where?"

She offers a small smile. "Annika's Apex."

Despite the long P.S. I'd added to the end of my note, part of me still wondered whether Elinor would want to contribute to a plan designed to really hurt her aunt. Apparently, she would.

"I don't know," I say. "I'm not really supposed to leave, and the GS will be here soon and—" I stop myself. What am I talking about? The prettiest girl I've ever seen might've forgiven me *and* has risked who knows what to break me out of jail. I've already done things no Troublemaker has done before and found out that Kilter's idea of serious punishment is some people's idea of a dream vacation. What's the worst that can happen?

"Let me get my coat," I say.

Solitary confinement is located on the top floor of the dorms. And as it turns out, its door is the biggest obstacle to escaping. It's locked by a series of cards and passwords, all of which Elinor has and knows. When I ask how, she repeats that she has her ways. I pull my jacket hood low over my eyes as we run down the hallway, which is surprisingly unprotected by GS, down three flights of stairs, and outside. A Kilter Series 7000 scooter with attached sidecar waits at the back of the building.

"Bows and arrows and two Boomarees," Elinor says, hopping on the scooter. "That's all the Kommissary had left."

She's referring to the weapons in the sidecar. They're nestled in with tubes of paint, lighters, matches, kindling, protective vests, and face shields.

"I don't think I'll fit," I say.

She scoots up. "Sure you will."

It takes me a second to realize she wants me to sit behind her. Like, on the same seat. Probably with my hands around her waist.

"Would you rather drive?"

"Nope." I hop on and take the helmet she hands to me. I peer over her shoulder as she fiddles with the digital map. I've just buckled the helmet strap when she hits "Annika's Apex." I have just enough time to grab the sides of her coat before the scooter zooms away.

Like our last trip up the mountain, the scenery flies by in blue, green, and brown squiggles. The air's cold and the wind stings my eyes; I'd close them but I'm afraid of missing something important—like Capital T driving back to campus, their mission complete. Plus, I'm on a *scooter* with *Elinor.* This could very well be the best thing that ever happens to me, and I want to commit every single second to memory.

When we reach the mountain and the scooter shoots up a snowy trail, I realize I still haven't said what I need to out loud.

"I'm sorry!" I call over the rush of wind. And, "Thank you!"

"It's okay!" Elinor calls back. "And you don't have to thank me!"

"Are you kidding? After you were so nice? And I was such a loser? To break me out of—"

"I wasn't that nice!"

I'm about to protest when she yells again.

"There's no phone!"

I lean forward. "Excuse me?"

"A few weeks ago, when I said I knew where there was a real phone, and you followed me into the woods and across the river." She pauses as the scooter shoots up and over a fallen tree. "There was no phone. I lied!"

"There is a phone!" I shout. "I used it!"

The scooter slows slightly, briefly. "Well, if there is, I had no idea. Really!"

The scooter speeds up again. "Then why'd you lie?"

Her shoulder taps my chin as she shrugs. "That's what I do!"

We weave sharply through hanging branches. My arms tighten around her waist. "I thought you ran!" I yell. "You're always disappearing!"

"That's part of it! The longer I talk to someone, the more I get to know him. The more I get to know him, the harder it is to lie. So I leave to avoid telling the truth!"

I picture the Performance Pavilion, the tutor assignment ceremony. Elinor's tutor, the guy who tried to convince us he was a blind psychic. It's totally weird . . . but it also makes sense.

"What about the pictures?" I shout. "What were you doing with them that day in the gazebo?"

"History extra-credit assignment!"

Before I can ask anything else, the scooter jolts forward. We fly through the air for what feels like minutes and finally hit the ground with a thud. The scooter stops, and Elinor climbs off.

Still seated, I look past her. The iron arch is ten feet away. Snowflakes swirl through the cold air. An image of little Annika and her father walking under the arch flashes through my mind . . . and I wonder if this is such a good idea.

"Seamus."

I look down. Elinor's mittened hand is on my arm.

"She asked for this," she reminds me. "If Annika didn't want something like this to happen, she shouldn't have asked us to make her cry."

"I know." I still don't move.

A second later her fingers gently squeeze my arm. "Seamus?"

I look up. Her copper eyes are warm, reassuring.

"Your friends need you."

I let this sink in. Then I nod, slide off the scooter, and help gather weapons.

"I won't let them down. Not this time."

Chapter 25

DEMERITS: 3750
GOLD STARS: 830

As Elinor and I enter the Apex, it looks like Capital T's just getting started. Nothing's burned down or completely vandalized. Lemon's on his knees by the carousel, blowing on a small pile of lit twigs and paper. Abe stands before the rotting funnel cake stand, shaking a can of spray paint. Gabby appears to be searching for something as she weaves through rides and structures.

But as we walk closer, I see Lemon's furry eyebrows lowered so far down they practically meet his cheeks. Abe's arm trembles as he aims the can, like he's unsure of where and how to spray. Gabby's eyes are wide as she dashes forward, then backward, then forward again, like she's afraid she'll miss whatever it is she's looking for.

This isn't the same alliance that strode confidently into the darkness to bring down Mr. Tempest.

"Abort!" Gabby shrieks suddenly. "Abort, abort, *abort*!"

"What are you talking about?" Abe demands. "How can we abort when there's nothing to—"

He stops. Elinor and I stop. Lemon glances up from his flameless fire, follows Gabby's pointer finger, and stops. For several seconds, no one speaks. Then, feeling Elinor's elbow gently nudge my arm, I find my voice.

"We want to help."

"Thanks," Abe shoots back, "but we don't want you to."

My eyes flicker to him briefly, then shift to Lemon. "We have supplies. Paint and lighters and other stuff."

"Maybe you didn't hear me," Abe says. "We don't—"

Lemon holds up one hand. Stands. Walks toward us. Elinor and I hold out the bags of weapons so he can see what we have.

"Dude," Abe hisses, like Elinor and I aren't right there.

Lemon ignores him and peers into the bags. "The lighters are new?"

"Yes," Elinor says. "Fresh off Kommissary shelves."

He nods, peers some more. "Face shields might be useful." His eyes lift to mine. "The flames aren't holding in the snow and wind."

My chest warms. I nod too.

"Um, Lemon?" Abe calls out. "Can we talk for a second? Please?"

"Whatever you have to say, you can say here," Lemon calls back.

Abe's fists clench at his sides, his feet stand firm. I think he'll refuse, but then he takes a breath, so deep and loud we can hear it from fifteen feet away, and jogs toward us. Gabby jogs after him. When they reach us, Abe gives Elinor, then me, a big, fake smile and faces Lemon.

"Do I need to remind everyone what we learned about Teacher's Pet here? And *why* he's Teacher's Pet? Am I the only one who realizes this could be a huge trick? In case you've forgotten, we're on the top of a mountain in the middle of nowhere. If—*when*—he uses those weapons on us, it's not like anyone will hear our screams for help."

Lemon looks at him. "Are you done?"

Surprised by the question, Abe takes a second to nod.

"Then in case *you've* forgotten," Lemon says, "Seamus stuck by me when no one—and I mean *no one*—else did. I practically killed him a dozen times, and what did he do? He stayed. He tried to help. If he wanted to take me out, he could've—and for good reason. He didn't."

"But—"

Lemon cuts Abe off. Turns his gaze to me. "Then, when I didn't return the favor, when I gave up on him immediately without giving him a chance to explain, he stuck by me again. He's still . . . sticking by me." He shifts his eyes to Abe, then Gabby. "By *us*."

Abe pouts. Gabby frowns. Neither disagrees.

"People make mistakes. We *all* make mistakes. But what sets one person apart from the next is what he does afterward. In that way, Seamus has proven himself time and again." Lemon pauses. "Plus, I know he's sorry."

"So sorry," I chime in. "Really."

"Really," Elinor vouches. "I have the K-Mail to prove it."

This is followed by a long moment of silence. I'm getting ready to apologize again when Abe shrugs.

"I guess a little help wouldn't hurt," he says.

This, I learn when Lemon fills me in, is an understatement. With no credits to buy more supplies, the alliance members are relying on what they already had. After a semester of serious troublemaking, this amounts to dried-up colored contact lenses for Gabby, a single can of spray paint for Abe, a book of matches and some kindling for Lemon, and a canister of gasoline the group siphoned from Annika's golf cart before leaving campus.

"The original goal was to bring down the whole park," Lemon says. "But we revised the plan when we realized just how little we had to work with. Now the goal is to mess with a few of the smaller structures, mostly with spray paint, and burn down the carousel."

I nod. The carousel's the centerpiece of the park. If the destruction of any single attraction will make Annika cry, it's that one.

"Under normal circumstances I'd be able to light several small fires around the base that'd eventually run together and send the entire ride up in flames, but the weather's not cooperating." Lemon leads us to a small, blackened mound by the carousel's steps. "The snow makes a dry start nearly impossible, and when I finally get a few flames going, the wind blows them out."

"The lighters and face shields should help, right?" I ask.

He holds out one hand, palm side up. "That's the hope."

We get to work. Gabby resumes looking for hidden cameras that, if she finds, she'll either block or break to stall the GS and buy the group more time. Abe starts tagging game booths with capital *T*s. And using our bodies and face shields, Elinor and I form a wall to the wind as Lemon works with lighters and twigs.

But Mother Nature's strong. And today she's cranky, too. Lemon manages to start several fires, but each time we move on to start a new one, the old one blows out. We try lingering to give the flames a chance to grow, but we can do this only so long before the heat scalds our hands and faces. And that, unfortunately, isn't enough time for the fires to build up their defenses. Mother Nature snuffs them out, one by one by one.

After twenty minutes, Lemon sits back on his heels. Rests his hands on his thighs. Shakes his head.

"It's not going to happen," he says.

Unwilling to give up so soon, I search through the remaining supplies. They're all useful, but not necessarily for our current purposes. I'm considering how a staple gun and a roll of duct tape can help us when Gabby jogs up.

"No cameras," she says, breathless. "Just some weird buzzing box I thought might be a camera—but was just a weird buzzing box."

"That's okay," Lemon says. "We're not doing anything worth hiding from view anyway."

He stands. Calls Abe and motions for him to join us. Sensing we're about to raise the white flag of defeat, I scan the park, rack my brain for alternative approaches. As I'm thinking, my eyes pass over a large gray box attached to a tall wooden pole. Then, remembering what Gabby just said, they shoot back, zero in.

Abe's just reached us when I start jogging.

"Seamus?" Lemon says. "Where are you going?"

"I knew it!" Abe exclaims. "I knew he was trouble. Didn't I say he was—"

He's cut off, but I don't turn around to see how. I continue to the pole, then stop and listen.

Gabby's right. The box is buzzing. Like it contains a thousand angry bumblebees.

"What is it?" Lemon stands next to me.

I nod to the box. He looks up and listens.

"Electricity," we say at the same time.

Abe, Gabby, and Elinor come up behind us. When we tell them what the box contains, they all have questions.

"Are you sure?" Gabby asks.

"Didn't the last ride run, like, twenty years ago?" Elinor asks.

"What's the big deal?" Abe asks.

Lemon fields the first two. "Yes, we're sure. Look at the power lines connecting it to other poles throughout the park. And yes, the last ride ran a long time ago . . . but I guess they left the power on. Or forgot to turn it off."

"The big deal," I continue, "is that we can use the electricity to complete the Ultimate Troublemaking Task."

There's a pause. "How?" Elinor finally asks.

I think quickly. "The box stands higher than the carousel roof. If we can get it over there and blow it up, the shower of sparks it makes will be like lighting a million matches and lighters all at once."

"Okay," Abe says, sounding skeptical and pleased at the same time, "first, the box is attached to a pole twenty feet in the air. How are we going to get it from there to the carousel roof ten feet away? Second, how are we going to blow it up? Third, does it also control the snow and wind? Because if not, the sparks will still go out as fast as the matches and lighters did."

"The gasoline." Lemon nods as he puts it together. "That we took from Annika's golf cart. If we douse the roof with it, the sparks will land and catch before they can go out. The fire that results should be big enough to hold its own—and even spread to the rest of the ride."

"As for how we get the box from the pole to the roof," I say, "leave that part up to me."

Lemon quickly assigns other responsibilities, and we scatter. Using benches and fake horses for support, Abe, Gabby, and Elinor scale the carousel and climb onto the roof, where they start clearing off accumulated snow. Lemon arranges small mounds of twigs and kindling throughout the ride, then pours a few drops of gasoline on each. I retrieve the bag of weapons and search for a good firing spot, finally deciding on the top of a slide. It looks like the kind you'd find on a playground, but taller. And rustier, of course.

Once the carousel roof's cleared, Abe, Gabby, and Elinor climb down, and Lemon climbs up with the canister of gasoline.

He pours it over the entire surface, then jumps to the ground and gives me a thumbs-up.

I raise my loaded bow and arrow. Close one eye. Focus on the gray box ten feet away. Pull back my arm. Shoot.

And miss. The arrow flies past the box and lands silently in the snow below.

Abe groans. Lemon elbows him.

It's okay, I tell myself as I reload. *You're a little out of practice, but it's like riding a bike. Just stay calm.*

The next arrow nicks the bottom right corner of the box. The third hits the left side. The fourth slams into the front. The fifth nails the center, making the box shriek and wobble.

Perfect. Or it would be if I had any arrows left.

Down below, Lemon watches me steadily. Abe paces back and forth. Gabby and Elinor huddle together for warmth. Seeing them should make me more nervous, but instead I feel a strengthening surge of determination.

I take a Boomaree from the bag of supplies and remove the return sensor. With steady hands, I aim, bring back my wrist, and flick it forward. The Boomaree hits where the last arrow did, denting the metal and knocking the box so that it tilts forward.

I bring back the silver disc and try again. Another direct hit pushes the box some more and sends a dozen sparks shooting into the air.

I take the second Boomaree from the bag as the first returns. Then I pause, calculating distance and estimating force needed to propel the box from the pole to the carousel roof. It's a long shot. Longer than I thought it'd be. For one thing, I don't know how heavy the box is. There's a chance it could drop to the ground right next to the pole. For another, I was relying on the impact of the box hitting the roof to set off the required explosion. What if that doesn't happen?

As my palms begin to sweat inside my gloves, I look down at the group again. No one's moved besides Abe, who's clearly given up on me and is spraying the side of the ring-toss booth. I'm debating whether *I* should give up on me when my eyes catch the silver glint of the spray-paint can.

That's it.

I wave to Lemon and motion to Abe. Lemon catches on immediately, hurries to the ring-toss booth, and says something I can't hear. Ten seconds later he's at the base of the slide's ladder.

"Good luck," he says. And then he tosses up the spray-paint can.

I move quickly, automatically. I tear off pieces of duct tape and use them to attach the spray-paint can to the top of one Boomaree and the second Boomaree to the top of the spray-paint can. When I'm done, it looks like a giant aerosol Oreo.

Holding my breath, I aim. Focus. Turn back my wrist, bring my arm all the way across my chest . . . and fling it forward.

The Boomaree slams into the box. The spray-paint can explodes. The combined force sends the box flying off the wooden pole to the carousel roof, where it lands and detonates like a bomb—a real bomb, not one made for effective-yet-safe troublemaking.

The earth shakes. The ladder quivers. I try to hold on, but my gloves slip from the railings. I hit the ground with a thud.

At which point I'm pretty sure I'm dead. But then I manage to open one eye.

And watch a single tear slide down Annika's cheek.

"Congratulations, Seamus," she whispers. "You've successfully completed this year's Ultimate Troublemaking Task."

Chapter 26

DEMERITS: 5000
GOLD STARS: 830

Annika offers me a hand. I take it. As she helps me up, the rest of the park comes into view. Five Good Samaritans are already working on putting out the tall, flickering flames that engulf the carousel. The alliance members cheer. Ike, Houdini, Wyatt, Devin, Samara, Fern, Lizzie, and even Mr. Tempest stand by the iron arch. Except for our solved Mystery, everyone claps.

Annika leads me before the carousel. She's wearing a long, hooded ice-blue cape with matching gloves, furry white boots, and a furry white hat. Her hair trails past her shoulders in soft, loose waves. She's never looked prettier except for one thing.

"I'm crying," she says. "You made me cry."

"I'm sorry," I say automatically.

"Don't be." She sniffs, dabs at the corners of her eyes. "I've never been prouder."

I look at her, then behind me at the poor fake horses. They're missing noses, eyes, legs, and tails. Flames crackle and smoke swirls around them.

"You're crying because you're *proud*?" I ask. "Not because you're sad?"

"Why would I be sad? This place was a bad memory, nothing more. Now I get to remember it as something that helped a group of very talented Troublemakers further their careers."

She waves to the faculty members. The group parts in the middle and moves down, revealing a long table covered in silver platters, ice buckets, and champagne flutes.

"What's that?" I ask.

"Fish sticks, sparkling cider, and your alliance's favorite snacks." She waves at Lemon, Abe, and Gabby. "Don't worry! Though Seamus is responsible for the ultimate destruction of the carousel, we recognize that his actions wouldn't have been possible without yours."

"So we passed the task?" Abe asks.

"Indeed," Annika says. "With fewer demerits than your leader, but successfully all the same."

Abe and Gabby whoop, exchange high fives, and head for the snack table. Lemon, smiling, follows close behind. Still processing everything, I hang back with Annika.

"How'd you get here so fast?" I ask. "There were no security cameras. And I don't think any of us actually thought we were going to pull this off—at least, not until the very last second."

"Seamus." Annika smiles. Winks. "I have my ways."

Which is exactly what Elinor said when she broke me out of solitary confinement. And that reminds me . . . where *is* Elinor? She's not with the alliance members or our teachers. She's not with the Good Samaritans, either.

"It's like a snow globe."

As Annika heads toward the snack table, my head snaps to the right. Through the smoke and snow, I can barely make out a figure lying on the ground at the base of the carousel.

"Elinor." I run. Drop to my knees. Feel the blood leave my face. "Oh no—what—how—?"

She puts one blistered palm to my arm and lifts her chin.

"Isn't it?" she asks softly. "Like being in a snow globe?"

Between the thick flakes, light from the fires, and music someone's turned on near the snack table, yes, Annika's Apex looks like it should be under a shiny glass dome. But I can't think about that. All I can think about is Elinor's right hand and forearm, which are bare—because her mitten and sleeve have been singed off. Her skin looks like pink bubble wrap.

"Help!" I yell, yanking off my backpack. "She's hurt!"

The music grows louder as I fumble through my supplies. I don't know what I'm looking for. Duct tape? A fire extinguisher?

"Please!" I shout. "Elinor's been burned! She needs help!"

I turn the backpack upside down. The contents drop into the snow. As I sift through them, the music grows even louder. I glance behind me to see everyone still talking, laughing, and eating like nothing's wrong.

"Elinor." I lean toward her. Gently brush her hair off her face. "Don't move, okay? I'm going to get help."

She tries to smile. I make sure she's far enough away from the lingering flames and then sprint to the table.

"We need help," I gasp, knocking the iPod player to the

ground. The park falls silent. "Elinor's hurt. Badly."

Here's what I expect to happen: Annika, our teachers, and Capital T will drop their plates and run as fast as they can to our fallen Troublemaker. The Good Samaritans will beat them there and immediately start bandaging her burns. Annika will call for a helicopter that will swoop down in seconds and whisk Elinor away to the nearest hospital. Some of our teachers, and maybe Annika herself, will accompany Elinor so that she knows she's not alone. Once they're safely on their way, the rest of us will finish putting out fires and return to campus, where we'll anxiously await news.

Here's what actually happens: Lemon, Abe, and Gabby drop their plates and run as fast as they can to our fallen Troublemaker. Our teachers exchange concerned looks but don't move. Annika frowns as she peers past me, and then takes her K-Pak from the folds of her cape. She types quickly, replaces the K-Pak, and smiles at me.

"Thank you, Seamus. Elinor will be fine."

I glance behind me. One Good Samaritan—not even all five—jogs over to Elinor. He squats next to her and takes a handful of Band-Aids from his fanny pack.

I turn back. "That's it? She's really hurt. It's freezing up here. We need to get her off this mountain. *Now.*"

Annika still smiles, but she looks different. Her lips are pressed tighter together. Her eyes narrow. Her voice is cool when she takes a tall glass from the table, holds it toward me, and says, "Everything's under control. Why don't you have some sparkling cider and relax?"

My chin falls. This reaction to any injured student would be bad enough . . . but Elinor is Annika's *niece*. Annika should be so worried she has trouble running and barking orders—but she should run and bark orders anyway. How can she care so little about her own family?

I shake my head and shuffle backward. Slowly at first, then faster. I give Annika several seconds to change her mind, to somehow make this right. But instead she takes the iPod player from the ground and turns the music back on.

So I spin around and run. When I reach Elinor, she's sitting up. Her hand and arm are covered with Band-Aids. Capital T kneels in the snow around her. Lemon waits for the Good Samaritan to go off for more bandages, then leans toward me.

"I've had my share of burns," he whispers. "These aren't

life-threatening, but they do require immediate, professional treatment. We need to get her to our scooters. She can ride back down the mountain in the sidecar, and we'll get help from there."

I swallow and nod. It's all I can do.

They move quickly but carefully. I don't know if the adults will try to intervene, but for better or worse, they're too busy at their little party to pay attention. Elinor walks between Lemon and Abe, who each keep an arm around her for support. They weave through the food and game stands and hurry through the iron arch.

I stay behind. Partly because I'm too stunned to move, but mostly because I want to stop the adults if they realize the kids have left and try to make trouble.

Still in the snow where it fell after I turned my backpack upside down, my K-Pak buzzes. Keeping one eye on the festivities, I pick it up. I click on my K-Mail and open the new message.

> Dear Seamus,
>
> I'm so sorry it's taken this long to get back to you. I recently returned from a long vacation and am just now catching up on my e-mail.

In any case, I wanted to let you know that I'm so glad you wrote, and I really appreciate everything you said in your note. Being a teacher isn't always easy, and I know the same is doubly true about being a student.

That said, I hope you know that I'm not mad, or upset, or sad about what happened. You were very brave to try to help, and for that I'll always be grateful.

If you'd like to write me again, I'd be happy to do the same.

"Hey, Seamus!" Ike shouts from the table. "Who are you going to pick?"

I can't feel my face, but somehow it lifts up. If the adults have noticed that I'm the only Troublemaker left, they don't care. "What do you mean?"

"For your first real-world troublemaking combat mission!"

As Houdini, Wyatt, Devin, and the other faculty members smile and wave, I vaguely recall something Annika said about choosing one to accompany on a top secret assignment.

I don't answer. My face drops, and my eyes lock on five words at the bottom of the K-Pak screen.

With kind regards,
Miss Parsippany

Already missing Seamus and the Capital T's? Send them an e-mail . . .
Visit
MERITSOFMISCHIEF.COM

. . . and they just might get back to you!

TO: loliver@kilteracademy.org;
ahansen@kilteracademy.org;
gryan@kilteracademy.org
FROM: shinkle@kilteracademy.org
SUBJECT: Winter Break

Hey guys!

I'm missing the Kanteen's fish sticks already. This ride is sooo long. I'm glad I have my K-Pak to keep me busy. I'm bummed I won't see you for a while, but you can always shoot me an e-mail! I'll be here...

—Seamus